FINAL TOUCH

Other Books by Brandilyn Collins

Rayne Tour series

1 | *Always Watching*

2 | *Last Breath*

3 | *Final Touch*

Books for adults

Dark Pursuit

Exposure

Kanner Lake Series

1 | *Violet Dawn*

2 | *Coral Moon*

3 | *Crimson Eve*

4 | *Amber Morn*

Hidden Faces Series

1 | *Brink of Death*

2 | *Stain of Guilt*

3 | *Dead of Night*

4 | *Web of Lies*

Chelsea Adams Series

1 | *Eyes of Elisha*

2 | *Dread Champion*

Bradleyville Series

1 | *Cast a Road Before Me*

2 | *Color the Sidewalk for Me*

3 | *Capture the Wind for Me*

Brandilyn Collins & Amberly Collins

FINAL TOUCH

BOOK THREE

the Rayne Tour

ZONDERVAN®

ZONDERVAN

Final Touch
Copyright © 2010 by Brandilyn Collins

This title is also available as a Zondervan ebook.
Visit www.zondervan.com/ebooks.

Requests for information should be addressed to:
Zondervan, 3900 *Sparks Dr. SE, Grand Rapids, Michigan* 49546

This edition: ISBN-978-0-310-74959-2

Library of Congress Cataloging-in-Publication Data

Collins, Brandilyn. -
    Final touch / Brandilyn Collins & Amberly Collins.
       p. cm. — (The Rayne Tour ; bk. 3)
    Summary: Minutes before her rock-star mother is to marry her once-estranged
father and make her life complete, sixteen-year-old Shaley is kidnapped, and she
must stay strong and rely on God to help her save herself.
    ISBN 978-0-310-71933-5 (softcover)
    [1. Kidnapping — Fiction. 2. Fame — Fiction. 3. Rock groups — Fiction. 4. Christian
life — Fiction.] I. Collins, Amberly. II. Title.
PZ7.C692Fi   2010
[Fic] — dc22   2010008414

Any Internet addresses (websites, blogs, etc.) and telephone numbers in this book are offered as a resource. They are not intended in any way to be or imply an endorsement by Zondervan, nor does Zondervan vouch for the content of these sites and numbers for the life of this book.

Published in association with the literary agency of Alive Communications, Inc., 7680 Goddard Street, Suite 200, Colorado Springs, CO 80920. www.alivecommunications.com

Interior design: Christine Orejuela-Winkelman

Printed in the United States of America

15 16 17 18 19 20 21 22 /DCI/ 20 19 18 17 16 15 14 13 12 11 10 9 8 7 6 5 4 3 2 1

Dear Reader,

Great to see you back for another book in the Rayne Tour series, featuring Shaley O'Connor. *Final Touch* is the third book in the series. This story can be read on its own, but we do hope you've first read books one and two — *Always Watching* and *Last Breath*. If you know everything that Shaley's been through, you'll enjoy *Final Touch* all the more.

This story takes place almost a year after the events of *Last Breath*. Just when Shaley thinks everything in her life is finally coming together, the unimaginable happens.

We'd love to hear from you after you've read this book. If you drop by Brandilyn's website at *www.brandilyncollins.com*, you can email us from there.

~ *Brandilyn and Amberly Collins*

PART 1
Saturday

’ve been dreaming of this day my whole life!"

My mom and my long-lost father were finally marrying. For the first time, we'd be a family — a *real* family, living under the same roof. From now on I could come home from high school to a mom *and* a dad. How I'd begged God for this. How I'd yearned for it, ever since I was little and wondered where my father was. *Who* he was. Now I wanted to shout and sing and dance.

And I would, except, as maid of honor, I was dressed to the nines in beautiful coral silk, and I didn't dare get sweaty.

Instead I gently cupped my hands around Mom's cheeks. We smiled at each other. Then my throat started to tighten. *Uh-oh.* My mouth wavered, and so did Mom's. Tears filled our eyes.

"Oh, no!" I pulled back and waved my hands in the air. "No, no, no, I *do not* want to cry!"

We both were fully made up, as were the other bridesmaids in the room, Brittany and Kim. The wedding would start in forty-five minutes. This was not the time to mess up our mascara.

"Here, Shaley." My best friend, Brittany, thrust a tissue into my hand, then gave one to my mom. That's Brittany — always ready. "Blot. Carefully."

Mom and I smiled lopsidedly at each other as we pressed the tissues to the corners of our eyes.

I've seen my mom glamoured up for countless concerts and interviews. But I've never seen her so beautiful. Mom's designer wedding gown fit tightly at her slim waist, with beading all over, even on the long, satiny train. Coral-colored pearls rimmed the edges. Mom's blonde hair swept upward, a flower-topped veil hanging all the way to the floor as a gossamer layer over the train. She looked stunning. And not just because her makeup and hair were perfect. Because she was so happy on the inside. Gary Donovon, the high-school sweetheart who'd been wrenched from her life eighteen years ago, would become her husband today.

"Looks good." Kim, keyboard player for Mom's rock band — named Rayne after Mom — smiled as she took the tissue from my mother's hand and threw it away. "No more tears now."

Mom shook her head, her face lit with joy. "No more tears."

"What time is it?" Kim checked the clock in the huge bedroom, and my eyes followed. Three twenty. Forty minutes seemed like forever to wait.

We were in an incredible castlelike house and property covering eleven lush acres outside Santa Barbara, California. It was a second home belonging to movie producer Ed Schering, a friend of Mom's. The ceremony would take place in the house's seventy-foot-long great room. The reception would spill out to the gardens.

Ed had offered the estate as a secure, gated place for the wedding. No media could get near the place — unless they tried by helicopter. Which I wouldn't put past them, once they sniffed us out. The media had dubbed Mom and Dad's upcoming ceremony the "wedding of the century," but so far the date had remained secret from the public.

"Dad's ring had better come." I sidled to a window overlooking the rear gardens of the estate and nudged back a curtain. The person delivering the ring was supposed to swing around the driveway to the kitchen's back door, where I'd meet him. That ring was my responsibility. During the ceremony I'd carry it until giving it to Mom to put on Dad's finger.

Mom sighed — a quick breath of nervousness and excitement. "I don't want to go through a honeymoon without a wedding ring on my husband's finger." She faced herself in a full-length mirror and patted her already-perfect hair.

I moved to my cell phone, sitting on a dresser. "Maybe I should call the store."

Dad's custom wedding ring had been made too small — a surprising mistake for such well-known jewelers. We'd only discovered the mistake yesterday, when both wedding rings were delivered to our house in Southern California and Dad's didn't fit. We were just about to leave for the rehearsal at the estate, and the only thing we could do was contact a jewelry store in Santa Barbara this morning for a last-minute sizing. Wendell, one of Mom's bodyguards, had taken the ring to the store. The owners promised to resize it and send it back with a driver before the ceremony.

Which was now in thirty-five minutes.

Just as I picked up my cell phone, it rang. I checked the ID. *Gary Donovon.*

I pressed the button to answer. "Hey, Dad."

Seeing my dad's name felt good. For years he'd gone by a legal alias to protect himself and my mom. Since coming to Southern California, my father had taken back his original name. My mom liked that — it was the name she'd always known him by.

"Hi. How're all my girls over there?"

"Over there" meant on this side of the two-story great room. The men's dressing area was in a bedroom on the other side. Twin curving marble staircases rose to this second level, with a balcony and gilded railing running all the way around, providing a downward view into the magnificent great room. For the ceremony the men would go down the set of stairs on their side and line up below. We women would use the staircase on our side.

"We're fine. Mom's getting nervous. And we're still waiting for your ring."

"No sweat, we've still got plenty of time."

That sounded like my dad — laid-back, hard to rattle.

"Hear the noise out there, Shaley? I've peeked out. People are gathering, wanting a show."

Friends had come from all over, and I knew there would be

quite a few recognizable faces from the music industry. All had been asked not to tell anyone where the wedding was taking place.

I smiled. "Rayne never fails to give 'em a show."

"Don't I know it."

"The guys all ready?" Morrey, the drummer for Rayne, and Rich, the bass player, were Dad's two attendants. Morrey, Kim's boyfriend, was best man. Ross, Rayne's manager, was also in their room, as well as Stan, Rayne's lead guitarist. Ross and Stan would meet Mom at the bottom of the stairs, one on either side, and give her away.

"We're ready and bored," Dad said. "Let's just start now, get this thing over with."

"Dad!" I pulled the cell from my ear and gave Mom a look. "He says he wants to get this thing over with."

Mom cocked her head and raised an eyebrow. Brittany shot me an *oh, good grief* look.

"Hey." Dad's voice filtered through the phone. "I didn't mean it like that!"

I laughed. "Then you're just going to have to wait."

"Okay, okay. But I'm tired of pacing around. I'm about to call Wendell to bring up a deck of cards."

"Believe me, once you see Mom come down those stairs, it'll be worth the wait."

He made a sound in his throat. "I bet she's gorgeous."

"Double gorgeous. You're gonna fall over just seeing her."

"You're killing me! That's it, no more waiting. Let's do this thing now."

I rolled my eyes at Mom. "I'm hanging up on you, Dad."

My finger punched the *end* button. I set my cell phone back on the dresser.

"Hey, Shaley." Brittany pointed to the flowers in her hair. "You still have to put yours on."

"Oh, I forgot." I hurried to the table we'd set up along the wall. All of our bouquets lay upon it, resplendent in shades of coral and white. My hair accessory lay beside them. Each bridesmaid's hair piece was made of three rosebuds, one coral to match our dresses, and two white—a special symbol between Mom and Dad of their love.

"Want some help?" Brittany asked.

"No, I've got it."

As I fiddled with attaching the flowers to the right side of my swept-up hair, I could see Kim and Brittany in the mirror's reflection. "Might as well save our feet," Kim said. She and Brittany sat down on the oversized bed. "You want to sit, Rayne?"

Mom spread her hands. "In all this?"

"We'll help you. Take that big armchair."

Kim and Brittany moved to help Mom back up to the chair. They lifted her veil, lowering her slowly down to sit on the train without wrinkling it. The veil they draped over the back of the chair. Satisfied, they sank back down on the bed.

There. The flowers felt secure in my long brown hair. The beautiful rosebuds were the final touch. I surveyed myself in the mirror. My eyes, blue like Mom's, were clear now, and the makeup hadn't smeared. The dress, hitting just above my tanned knees and with a bow in back, fit great. I still had to put my matching coral heels on, but I'd do that last minute.

Nothing more for me to do. But I couldn't sit. Like my dad, I could only pace and check the clock.

Twenty-five minutes.

Excitement pinged around inside me. And worry. *Where* was that ring?

My cell phone went off. I snatched it up and checked the ID. Frowned. "Who's this?" I read off the number.

"That's local," Mom said. "Maybe it's the ring."

I answered the call. "Hi, this is Shaley."

"This is Luke Walsh, security guard down at the gate. We just let Pogh Jewelers' van through with the ring. The guard up at the house will wave him around to the back."

"Oh, thanks!" I tossed my phone onto the bed and turned to Mom. "The ring's here!"

Relief showed on her face.

"Want me to go?" Brittany slid off the bed.

"No, it's okay. I'm getting that ring and then not letting it out of my sight." Still barefoot, I headed for the bedroom door. "Back in a flash."

Once in the hall I veered left, toward a back staircase that led down to a maid's quarters and the huge kitchen. I wound my way through the kitchen and the busy catering crew preparing for the reception. "You lost?" a woman asked me.

"Nope." I smiled. "Just picking up something."

Off the kitchen sat a pantry and a short hall leading to a back door, through which all party supplies were unloaded. Apparently Ed Schering threw a lot of parties.

I stepped outside to a sunny afternoon, the driveway pavement warm beneath my feet. At that moment a white van with *Pogh Jewelers* on the side appeared around the corner. It stopped about twenty feet away from me. At first I waited, thinking the driver would come a little closer. But when he opened the door, engine running, I went out to meet him.

"Hi. Thanks for coming." I half squinted at him, the sun in my eyes.

"No problem." The driver wore a baseball cap pulled low over his forehead. He dipped his chin in a nod but never raised his eyes to mine. I caught the merest glimpse of his face as he strode past me toward the rear of the van. "I got it back here."

A little ring box stuck in that big back area? Odd, but whatever. I just wanted to get it and go back inside. "Okay."

I followed him behind the van and stood back as he opened the double-wide doors. He glanced to the right, then left. I caught a quick look at his profile. He was ... maybe in his fifties? Low-hanging jowls and pudgy. His eyes were small, his lips full. Something about him looked familiar.

Have I seen this guy before?

Quickly, he leaned into the van and picked up something. Swung around.

He jumped toward me and hooked an arm around my neck.
Wha—?

His arm tightened.

I struggled. Opened my mouth to scream.

A large cloth smashed against my nose and lips. "You're mine now, Shaley." His words spit like fire.

No. No! I gasped in moist air and choked. Tried to hold my breath. My feet kicked, my arms swung.

The world wavered and dimmed.

Terror shot through me. My eyes opened wide. I fought with all my might. The man pressed the cloth harder against my face.

In a flash I saw the back of the van — empty. No ring box.

My muscles turned to water. I sank against the man's chest like an unstrung puppet.

Then blackness.

Where's Shaley?" Brittany pushed off the bed and peered out the window to the rear gardens. She couldn't see the driveway, where Shaley was supposed to pick up the ring. "She's been gone for seven minutes."

Rayne sat in the chair, back straight. Her long red fingernails drummed against the chair's arms. Clearly she was becoming more nervous about the ceremony with each passing minute. "She'll be here. Maybe she stopped in some bathroom. Heaven knows there are enough of them in this house."

Kim touched her white-blonde hair. "Maybe she saw someone she knows and stopped to say hi."

"But guests are coming in the front door to the great room." Brittany leaned toward the right side of the window to gaze as far left as possible. She still couldn't see the driveway. "She wouldn't be walking through there now."

"Don't worry." Rayne waved a hand in the air. "I don't think she'll miss the wedding."

Five minutes passed. No Shaley.

Something inside Brittany whispered dark thoughts.

Often in the past she'd had the ability to sense when something bad was coming. An inexplicable feeling in her gut. Brittany bit the side of her lip, telling herself not to listen this time. What could happen? They were on this beautiful estate with security guards everywhere, plus Rayne's three personal ones. Mick and Wendell had worked as bodyguards for Rayne for quite a few years. Both of them had been a lot of help during all the trauma a year ago. And Lee, whom Rayne had hired to replace Bruce after he was killed, had now been with the family for almost a year.

The ominous feeling within Brittany expanded, like a sponge soaking up black water. She glanced at the clock. Only thirteen minutes until the ceremony. "I'm going to find her."

She slipped out of the room before anyone could stop her.

Barefoot, she hurried down the back stairs and into the kitchen, where she saw three women from the catering service. Brittany pulled up short. "Did you see Shaley come through here?"

"Yeah, about ten minutes ago." A plump woman turned from the sink. "Went through that door." She pointed toward the pantry.

"Thanks." Brittany scurried toward the door.

Outside she blinked in the bright sun. Looked around. No sign of a delivery vehicle or Shaley. And not a soul in sight to ask.

Brittany hugged herself, suddenly cold in the warm afternoon.

Maybe Shaley was around the side of the house. That had to be it.

She started to walk up the driveway — and stopped after three strides. Her eyes riveted to a spot of coral and white about twenty-five feet away.

Shaley's hair flowers.

Brittany ran toward them, feet slapping against the asphalt. She skidded to a halt and stared down, trembling. The rosebuds were smashed and dirty. As if they'd been stepped on.

No. No, no, no. Shaley would never leave her hair arrangement like that.

Not far away, something caught Brittany's eye. She leaned over and picked it up.

A broken fingernail tip, French-manicure style. Shaley's.

The fat black sponge inside Brittany solidified and sank like a rock through her stomach.

She shook her head hard. *No!* There would be an explanation. Shaley was just around the corner. Surely, she was ...

Brittany dropped the fingernail and raced up the driveway.

Darkness swarmed around me, vibrating and smothering. Blanketing my head, then crumbling ... blanketing ... crumbling.

My eyes opened.

Still dark.

I blinked. Shifted my head.

My neck hurt. And my left cheek and eye.

I lay on my right side.

Where —

The wedding!

I gasped. Tried to sit up. My head hit something. Pain shot through my skull, and I collapsed back down.

Memories flooded. Meeting the van. The driver attacking me. His arm around my neck. Fighting him.

But this wasn't the van. I'd seen the back of it, large and empty. Where *was* I?

Beneath me the floor rocked. I blinked again, forcing my eyes to adjust. I reached out my left hand and felt metal. Dropped my hand to the floor, fingers exploring.

Rubber?

All my senses gelled at once. *Car trunk.*

No!

I cried out. Thrashed around, fear sucking the air from my lungs. How did I get from the van to this car? My arms hit the roof, the sides of the trunk. My dress tangled around my legs.

"Let me out! Let me *out!*" I banged on the roof until my fists hurt. Kicked with my bare feet. "Let me *ooouuutt!*"

Nothing moved. Nothing gave way.

Still I screamed and hit and kicked — on and on, until all my energy drained away.

I melted against the floor, breathing hard.

A thousand thoughts filled my head. The wedding. Mom. Dad. What were they thinking? They must be going crazy right now, looking for me.

The van driver. I thought I'd seen him before. Who was he? Why did he do this? *Why?*

This had to be a nightmare. Any minute now I'd wake up in Ed Schering's mansion. It would be the morning of the wedding...

Panic shoved its fingers down my throat. I couldn't breathe. I was going to *die.*

Screams tore from my mouth. Once again I pounded and raged, begging to be let out. What if other drivers on the road had their windows down? Would they hear me?

I yelled louder. Kicked harder. This time my energy didn't last as long. Soon my veins felt like they were filled with water. My knuckles and arms and legs throbbed. I brought fingers up to my face and felt something sticky.

Blood.

No more strength in me to fight. None. And no one to help. What was going to happen?

I would die here. I. Would. *Die.* Here.

I sank against the floor of the trunk and sobbed.

Brittany raced around the corner of the house. No Shaley. Heart in her throat, she sprinted up the driveway and rounded the corner to the front of the building. Down the length of the mansion she saw parking attendants and last-minute guests. Mick and Wendell stood at either side of the wide marble porch. They were dressed in suits for the wedding, but Brittany knew they carried guns at their waists. Radios were attached to their lapels.

Still no Shaley.

Brittany ran toward the bodyguards. "Wendell! Mick!" Her yells pierced the air. Guests turned.

Both men's heads snapped in her direction. Instantly they hurried toward her. Wendell reached her first. "What is it?" His deep-set eyes scanned her face, the bare feet. The sun shone on his spiky, gelled black hair, turning it almost purple. Wendell was short for a bodyguard, only five eleven. But he was muscular and hard-bodied, and Brittany knew he would stake his life to guard Rayne and Shaley.

"Sh-Shaley ..." Brittany couldn't force the words out.

Mick pulled up beside Wendell. He was taller, a former Marine. "Brittany, what's the matter?"

"Shaley's gone."

Mick gave her one of his squinty-eyed looks. "What do you mean, gone?"

"She was supposed to pick up the ring around back. Did you see a delivery truck?"

Alarm creased Wendell's face. "A van. We waved it on down there. It came back up a minute later."

"It's gone?" Brittany's throat tightened. "Shaley never came back to our room. And down where she was supposed to meet the van I saw her hair flowers on the ground. Crushed. And a broken fingernail!"

For a split second both bodyguards stared at her, openmouthed.

They broke into action, both running down the driveway toward the back of the house. Brittany raced after them.

They rounded the corner, Brittany now sweating. Strands of her once perfectly put-up hair fell against her neck. As they pulled up before the flowers, Brittany pointed. "See?"

Mick squatted down and looked at them, then pointed a thick finger at Shaley's broken nail. He twisted his head up and locked eyes with Wendell.

Mick searched the ground around the area. He stilled. Pointed again. "Is that blood?"

Blood? Brittany gasped. She leaned over, telling herself no. It was something else. *Anything* else.

She saw two little drops. Red.

She reared up and backed away, palms out. If it hadn't been for the trauma a year ago — the two murders, Shaley nearly killed, Rayne hit by a car — Brittany could have convinced herself this wasn't real. But life hadn't been the same since. Tragedy *could* happen, even with bodyguards all around.

Not a word could squeeze from Brittany's throat.

Wendell grabbed his radio. "Front gate, come in."

"Front gate here."

"That delivery van for the ring. Is it gone?"

"Yeah. A while ago."

"Did you check in the back before you let it out?"

The question hung in the air. Mick stood up. Brittany couldn't move.

"No." The security guard at the front gate sounded surprised.

"We checked it when it came in. We knew it was expected."

Wendell's jaw hardened. "Shut the gate. Don't let anyone else in or out. All other guards — be on the alert. Shaley's missing."

But it's too late, Brittany thought. The van was already gone.

Mick whipped out his cell phone and punched in 9-1-1.

5

I lay on my back in the car trunk, no more tears to cry. No more energy. My hands and arms and feet throbbed from trying to beat my way out. My neck hurt where the man had grabbed me, and my left cheek ... Had he hit me there? That side of my face was so tender. And my left eye felt swollen.

How much time had passed? I didn't know how long I'd been unconscious, or how long I'd been awake. Nothing made sense. The minutes drifted in and out, the car drove on and on, and darkness tried to swallow me whole.

My mind barely functioned. It couldn't comprehend anything at all. How did I get from the day of my dreams — to *this*?

I thought of Mom and Dad. Brittany. They had to be out of their minds with worry. Had they figured out what happened?

God, please help them. Help me. Let me live. Let me get back to them —

The car stopped.

My muscles tensed. I lifted my head up, and pain shot through my neck. My head sank back down.

My heart beat so hard it shook my body. Breath backed up in my throat.

I heard a car door slam.

Were those footsteps? Coming around to the back?

Some noise. A key in a lock?

My roof opened up, and a man loomed over me. Light stabbed my eyes. I whimpered and squeezed them shut.

Rough hands pulled me up. I tried to scramble away toward the back of the trunk. My arms lashed out.

"Stop it!" It was the voice of the man from the van. I looked up, trying to see his face. He grabbed me by the neck with one hand.

A long white cloth — pillowcase? — came down over my head.

"Fight me again and I'll make you sorry," he spat. "Hear me?"

I managed a nod but didn't know if he'd see it under the cloth. "Y-yes." My throat felt like sandpaper.

"That's a good girl." His hands moved to my sides. "Now get out."

The cloth over my head was thin, allowing light to seep in. I just could make out his form, towering over me.

Fear layered me in a cold sweat. What was he going to do to me? Would he kill me right here? "Wh-what do you want? Where are we going?"

"Shut up."

He pulled me awkwardly over the lip of the trunk. I started to fall, but he caught me. He righted me and lowered my shaking legs to the ground, then turned me around. "Walk straight ahead."

My ankles barely held me. I stumbled. He grabbed my arm and held me up. Pain tore from my wrist to my shoulder.

"Ah!" I shrank away.

"What's the matter with you? I'm just trying to help."

He'd kidnapped me, and he thought he was trying to *help*? What kind of crazy man was this? "My arm hurts."

"What?" He grasped my hands, hurting me more. Air hissed through my teeth. The man turned my hands over in his, as if examining them. I peered downward, seeing only my bare feet on grass, and the tip of one worn brown shoe.

"You did this to your own hands." He sounded disgusted. His shoe moved out of my sight.

Like this was *my* fault.

"Trying to get out didn't work too well, did it? All you've done is bruised yourself up. *Don't* do that again."

As if *he* hadn't bruised me at all.

"Move." He pushed me forward. I stumbled along, watching grass slide by beneath me.

"Stop." He yanked me to a halt. I felt him move around me. Heard the click of a car door opening. The pillowcase was pulled off my head.

I blinked. Before me lay the dirty beige interior of a big SUV.

"Get in." He pressed against my spine. "Go back to the third row."

Everything in me wanted to run. But where would I go? He'd catch me in a few steps. My legs weren't strong enough to take me anywhere.

I struggled up the step and into the SUV. Moved behind the long second-row seat and toward the third.

"Lie down on the floor."

The floor carpet was dusty and stained. "There's not much room."

"*Do* it."

Tears filled my eyes. Why had God let this happen to me?

I lay down on my left side, head resting on my arm — and cried.

The door slammed shut. Seconds later the driver's door opened. I heard the swish of clothes, a seat creak as my kidnapper got in.

The engine started.

He drove forward. I felt a little bump as the wheels hit pavement. He turned left and we sped up, taking me farther away from my life and family.

With Mick still on the phone to 9-1-1, Brittany ran through the back door into the kitchen, shouting, "Has anybody seen Shaley? Has *anyone* seen Shaley?"

The caterers stopped their work, eyes wide. "She didn't come back through here," one of them replied.

Brittany barely stopped. She careened past the women, into a hall, through the dining room, headed for the great room. Over the slap of her own bare feet she could hear the chamber orchestra playing, the rustle of guests. Lee, Rayne's newest bodyguard, hurried toward Brittany through a passage leading to the arched entrance of the great room. The overhead light shone on his shaved black head. Brittany pulled to a stop, breathing hard. "Have you seen Shaley?"

His dark eyes searched her face. "No. I've checked this area and in the great r — "

Ed Schering appeared, concern etching his lined forehead. He pressed a hand to the lapel of his black tuxedo. "What's going on? The guests just coming in are whispering about Shaley."

"She's gone." Words flooded from Brittany in one jumbled sentence. "I think the van driver took her Mick called the police I saw her flowers and there's blood."

"*What?*"

No time to explain. The wedding was supposed to be starting. Brittany whirled and ran toward the back staircase. She had to get to Rayne.

How to tell her? Brittany's mind screamed as she pounded up the steps. How to tell Rayne Shaley was *gone*?

But she wasn't gone. Not really. Any minute now they'd find her. Somewhere.

Brittany burst into the second floor hallway. At the door to the bedroom she stopped, dragged in a breath. She had to be calm for Rayne.

She pushed open the door. Rayne's head swung toward Brittany, eyes widening as she saw Brittany's disheveled hair, the sweat and fear on her face. Rayne rose instantly. "What's wrong? Where's Shaley?"

"I don't know. She's — " Brittany's throat swelled shut.

Time spun into chaos. Rayne pulled the horrible information from Brittany and snatched up her cell phone. She called Mick, who confirmed what he'd seen. Rayne ripped off her veil and pressed both hands to her mouth as Kim unsnapped her train. She ran out of the room and down the wide, open passage spanning the length of the balcony, not even glancing at the guests below, who were straining their necks up to watch. Brittany followed. Around past the first curving staircase they went. All the way across the connecting balcony, past the second staircase. Around the corner and down the hall to the room where the men were waiting. Rayne flung the door open. "Gary, Gary!"

In seconds, Brittany spilled her story once again. She couldn't bear to look at Rayne and Gary. Rayne so beautiful, so perfect, made up for her wedding, now clutching her beaded gown in disbelief. Gary, tall and handsome in his tux, holding Rayne, telling her everything would be all right. His gray eyes looked terrified. Like Brittany, they both knew how quickly tragedy could strike. Morrey, Rich, Stan, and Ross crowded around, firing questions.

Ross barreled toward the door. Everyone else piled out after him, hurrying down the nearest staircase. Guests now stood up, clamoring to know what was happening. Brittany ran along with Rayne, Gary, and the others past the guests and down the length of the great room, headed for the back of the house. She understood their wanting, *needing* to see the rear driveway, Shaley's flowers, the hope that if they viewed the scene they would see that it wasn't real, and Shaley would be right there.

If only it could be true.

Ed Schering paced through the lushly flowered great room, calling for all the guests to take their seats and be calm.

Before Brittany, Rayne, and Gary reached the back doors opening out to the gardens, two deputies from Santa Barbara County Sheriff's Department strode through the front entrance. Then there were questions and more questions, Brittany telling what she saw, breaking into tears as she led the deputies to the rear driveway, pointing to that awful, terrible place on the asphalt. She heard Rayne saying, "No, no, no," and saw Gary shoving his fingers into his sandy hair.

"We'll find her," he declared. "She's here somewhere, we'll find her."

When the deputies stretched yellow crime-scene tape to cordon off the rear driveway, Rayne and Gary collapsed into each other's arms and cried.

I lay in a fetal position, face pressed nearly underneath the seat in front of me. My arms still hurt, as well as my hands and left cheek. Half of my fingernails were broken off, most likely lying in the trunk of that car. Dried blood flecked my hands. My left eye throbbed.

The kidnapper drove on and on. My mind hovered over one thought after another, not knowing where to land, what to believe.

I was so thirsty. And I had to go to the bathroom. Plus, my bare shoulders and legs were cold.

Long ago I'd untied the bow at my back, giving myself more room in my dress. The beautiful bridesmaid dress was ruined. Bloody. Dirty. Sweaty.

What time was it? I tilted my head up, wincing at the pain. The sky looked dusky. Had the sun set?

Where was he taking me? And *why*?

But in my heart I knew why. I'd been kidnapped for money. The ransom would be huge.

It wouldn't matter. Mom and Gary would pay it.

All I had to do was hang on. Be strong. Stay alive. Once the ransom was paid, I could go home.

Home. Already it seemed light-years away.

I struggled to swallow. My throat was so dry.

"I need water." It was the first time I'd dared speak since lying on his filthy floor.

No answer.

"I need water!"

"You'll have to wait."

"I can't wait. And I have to go to the bathroom."

"Another hour, we'll stop."

"I can't wait that long."

No answer.

I pled. My captor refused to reply. Finally I fell silent, too tired to say any more.

We drove.

I prayed. Begged God to save me, to keep Mom and Dad strong. And Brittany. And everyone in the band. And Mitch and Lee and Wendell.

And, Lord, show me how to hang on until the ransom is paid.

Endless minutes ticked by. My bladder ached, and my head pounded. As the miles slipped beneath the SUV's wheels, I fell upon a chant to keep myself sane: *When he gets his money, he'll let me go home. When he gets his money, he'll let me go home.*

The sky darkened. My world on the car floor fell into deep shadow, then near blackness.

When I thought I could stand it no more, the SUV slowed and turned.

"Here." Something soft, thrown over the seats, hit me in the head. Then a second bundle landed on me. "Put these on."

I sat up. We drove more slowly, lights from businesses filtering into the car. I held the pieces of clothing up, squinting at them. A pair of jeans. A man's white undershirt.

"Hurry up," the kidnapper commanded.

With shaking hands I pulled my dress over my head. Slipped on the plain T-shirt. Every movement hurt. Slowly I scooted around, stuck my legs out straight on the floor and wiggled into the jeans. They were loose in the waist and too long. I rolled up the cuffs.

At least my legs were warmer.

The SUV turned again. Then stopped.

S even o'clock. It had been three hours since Rayne's life had fallen off a cliff.

In shock, Rayne slumped in the same armchair in which a lifetime ago she'd awaited her wedding. Her beautiful white, pearled dress now hung in the closet, along with the train and veil. She wore the jeans and blue top she'd put on that morning, before getting dressed for the ceremony. On the table at the far end of the room lay all the bouquets, slowly wilting.

I still can't believe this.

Everything had been so incredible this past year: Gary reentering Rayne's life. Falling in love with him all over again. Their engagement and plans to marry. Shaley was happier than she'd ever been. And, with Shaley's gentle prodding, both Rayne and Gary had turned to God, asking him to guide their new life together. God had given them a heavenly gift — each other — and both knew they'd mess up the marriage if God wasn't at the center of it. With Shaley by their side, they'd prayed and become Christians.

They were still so new at it, but wasn't God supposed to *bless* them for what they'd done? How could *this* happen?

Rayne watched Gary pace the room, unable to be still. Brittany, Kim, Morrey, Rich, Stan, and Ross sat in white chairs intended for the wedding guests, brought up from the great room. They, too, had changed out of their bridesmaid dresses and tuxes.

Rayne's and Gary's cell phones sat on a table near Rayne's chair.

The sheriff's department had wired both of them with portable recording devices in hopes that the kidnapper would call.

Both phones remained silent.

In the first hour following Shaley's disappearance, they had learned that Pogh Jewelers' van had been carjacked on its way to the estate. The driver had been knocked unconscious and left on the side of the road. He'd barely seen the face of his assailant. He would be in the hospital overnight for treatment.

Whoever stole that van had kidnapped Shaley.

Downstairs, many of the wedding guests still remained. One by one they were being questioned by the local sheriff's deputies. No one was being allowed to leave until questioned, Rayne had been assured of that. This location had been a secret. Did one of the guests have something to do with Shaley's disappearance?

Gary and Rayne couldn't believe that. But at this point, the sheriff's department would rule no one out.

Rayne stared at her phone, silently begging it to ring. Her eyes burned. Her body felt numb, like she'd gone to sleep and woken up in a thick, cold fog. She could barely move, yet she wanted to be *doing* something to find Shaley. But right now all they could do was wait. The local sheriff's department had called in the FBI for help, knowing this case would be highly publicized and require more manpower than their department could handle. An agent from the FBI's Los Angeles Field Office was on his way and would meet with the wedding party as soon as he arrived. Rayne was glad for all the help they could get, but they'd been expecting the agent for hours.

A *whop-whop* sounded overhead. Gary caught Rayne's eye. "Helicopter."

She managed a nod. "Think it's the sheriff's department or the media?"

"Probably the media. The sheriff's helicopters are out looking for the van."

"They should have found it by now." Morrey ran a hand through his shoulder-length black hair. One of his tattooed arms was around

Kim's shoulders. Morrey and Kim had been dating for a number of years. Rayne had thought their wedding would be next.

Now there would be no "next" anything. The world had stopped.

"Someone will find that van soon." Ross pressed a pudgy hand to his forehead. He sat forward in his chair, legs apart, staring at the floor. "The whole country's already looking for it."

The local sheriff's department had moved into swift action. Already they'd printed flyers of Shaley and were posting them around the area. A forensic artist was now interviewing the security guard who'd been at the front gate to create a drawing of the van driver's face. As soon as that was done, the drawing would be released to the media.

"How did he know?" Brittany's long blonde hair had long since fallen from its swept-up coiffure, and her makeup was streaked from tears. "The man who carjacked the van. How did he know Shaley was supposed to meet the driver — unless somebody at the jewelers told him? I mean, any one of us could have picked up that ring." Her voice dropped. "I wish *I* had."

"Brittany, you can't blame yourself." Kim's hair was down now as well, the flowers taken out. Her mascara and heavy blue eyeliner were smeared.

"No, you can't," Rayne whispered.

She'd done enough self-blaming of her own. If only she hadn't been so set on having that ring for the ceremony. If only she'd instructed one of her bodyguards to bring it upstairs. But Shaley had insisted she pick up the ring herself, since she was responsible for it during the ceremony. She'd called the jewelers that morning, reminding them to give it to no one but her. Now that seemed like such a silly thing for her to do.

But who could have known it would lead to this?

Rayne closed her eyes. "If it's anyone's fault, it's mine. I shouldn't have let her meet anyone without a bodyguard. *Why* did I do that?" She bent low, fresh tears stinging her eyes.

Gary knelt beside Rayne and drew her into his arms. "You couldn't have known. None of us could." His voice sounded flat. "This estate was so secure. We've been running around it since we got here last night. Shaley and Brittany didn't have a bodyguard with them every minute. We even had security watching the guests arrive."

"I know." Rayne cried in his arms. Her mind was about to crack in two. How was she going to stand another *minute* of this? "But still . . ."

Gary stroked her hair. "We'll find her. It'll be okay. We'll find her."

A knock sounded on the door. Rayne's head came up.

"Yeah," Ross called.

The door opened. A tall African-American man entered, dressed in slacks, a short-sleeved shirt, and tie. Around him hovered an energetic authority, as if his mere presence promised that something good would finally happen.

The FBI. Rayne stood on shaky legs.

"Miss O'Connor." The man nodded to her. He looked around forty, lean, with a long face and short-cropped hair. His eyes were hazel brown. "I'm Special Agent Al Scarrow." He shook Rayne's hand, then Gary's.

Hope flickered in Rayne's heart. "Thank you for coming."

Gary introduced the agent to everyone in the room.

Mick appeared at the door, carrying in a white chair for the agent. Al sat down. Gary pulled his chair close to Rayne.

Al leaned forward, hands clasped. He focused on Rayne. "I want you to know we're doing everything to bring Shaley back home. We've already got other agents from our office coordinating efforts with both the sheriff's department here and the Santa Barbara Police Department. Just before I got here I learned that the suspect composite is done. It's now being printed and will immediately be disseminated to the media."

"What about the van?" Gary's face looked tight and drawn.

"We've got units on the ground and in the air looking for that vehicle. We aim to find it, and soon."

Rayne nodded. Her mind still felt like it was wrapped in cotton. "We think the jewelers have something to do with this. They knew the ring was being delivered — " Her throat closed up.

Whop-whop. Again, a helicopter sounded overhead.

Al's eyes lifted. "That's probably a local TV station. Your location somehow leaked. Not surprising, with all the wedding guests leaving."

Bitterness rose within Rayne. "Why is a TV station so worried about getting a story *here*? They should help! They should be out looking for the van."

"I understand." Al pumped his clasped hands up and down. Rayne could tell his brain was jumping a dozen directions at once. "The media can be a real annoyance, but they can also be very helpful in getting the word out if used correctly. We've already got a spokesperson dealing with the media. Of course they want to know far more details than we're giving them right now."

"I'll bet." Rayne had her own love – hate relationship with the media. Especially the paparazzi.

At least her most-hated member of the paparazzi, Cat, had finally been convicted for stalking Shaley last year. In fact, Cat had been the first suspect Rayne thought of when Shaley disappeared. But the Santa Barbara County Sheriff's Department had checked. The man was just where he was supposed to be. In jail.

"Rayne was right earlier," Gary said. "The jewelers had to be in on this, or at least they told the wrong person. Whoever carjacked their van had to know the driver was meeting Shaley."

Al nodded. "We're taking a good look at that. We've got people interviewing the owners and employees of the store — " His cell phone rang.

Rayne jumped, even though she knew it wasn't her own cell. *Why* wouldn't hers ring?

"Excuse me." Al unclipped his phone from his belt, checked the ID, and answered. "Al Scarrow." He listened. Rayne's gaze glued to his face. She looked for any sign of news in his expression, but he gave away nothing. Wild frustration barreled through her. This agent was on their side. She and Gary *needed* him and all the forces behind him. But how could he be so *calm and controlled* about everything?

"Okay, thanks." Al ended the call and looked at Rayne. "They found the van."

As the SUV's engine cut off, I sat up. From the floor I could just see out the window. Sickly white overhead lights and gas pumps.

A service station.

There were few cars on the road running past the station. I leaned close to the window and looked far behind us. Were those signs for a freeway? Had we just come off of it?

Longing and fear and wild hope surged through me. How fast could I get to the other side of the SUV? Open the door and fling myself out? If I screamed, someone would hear me —

"Shaley," my kidnapper barked from the front seat. The sound of his voice drained the sudden energy from my limbs. Who was I kidding? If I so much as moved toward the door, that monster would be on me. Did I want to get beat up again?

"Shaley!"

I swallowed. "What?" My voice sounded dead.

"Put this on. Tuck your hair up in it."

A dirty blue baseball cap sailed over the seat in front of me and landed on my lap. It was the one he'd been wearing. I picked it up and stared at it stupidly. My thoughts jumbled together.

"You hear me?"

My bladder hurt so badly. I just wanted to get to the bathroom. Then get a drink of water. "Yes."

"Once you put that on, I'm going to come around and get you out. Take you inside to the bathroom. You're going to walk beside me and look down. You're not going to make a sound or talk to anyone. One word from you, and I'm yanking you back out of there. Got it?"

I studied the baseball cap. It said *San Diego* on the front. "Yes."

"You want to see your family again?"

"Yes!" The word caught in my throat. *Anything, I'll do anything! Just let me go home!*

"Then do what I say. Or you'll never see them again."

"Okay."

I pushed my hair up under the baseball cap. "Ready."

The driver's seat squeaked as he got out. I listened to his footsteps go around the front of the car. The door opened. "Come on. Hurry up."

I half scooted, half crawled toward the door. My whole body hurt. Shaking, I climbed out.

"Look down."

I did as I was told.

He gripped my elbow, shut the SUV's door, and walked me toward the station. Chin low, I sneaked looks right and left but saw no one.

We stopped. He opened the glass door, ushered me inside. Ahead of me I could see a row of shelves with chips and candy bars, but I heard no voices. The man veered right. I found myself in front of a door. He tried the handle, and it opened. "Go in." He kept his voice low. "Be quick."

I stumbled inside and headed for the toilet.

When I was done, I could barely stand up again. I forced myself to my feet and searched the room with my eyes. Was there a window somewhere? A vent I hadn't seen? Some way out other than going back to the man? Disappointed, I shuffled to the sink. Looked into the mirror. Breath backed up in my throat. My knees went watery. I grabbed onto the side of the sink as I gawked at the reflection.

Was that *me*?

Beneath the bill of the baseball cap, my left cheek and eye were red and swollen. Mascara and eyeliner had run in rivulets down my cheeks. My mouth turned down, lipstick smeared. I looked like a zombie.

Hatred and panic washed over me like a tidal wave. How had this happened? In just a few hours — look what I'd become. I'd landed on another planet, in another person's body. I didn't look like Shaley, feel like Shaley. I felt ... dead.

My mind drifted somewhere else. It couldn't stand to be there. My hands reached for the water, washed themselves of grime and blood. I bent over, cupped a palm, and took long drinks.

The next thing I knew I was outside the bathroom, the man's hand gripping my elbow once more. "Bend your head down." He walked me out of the building. I didn't see one other person. Somebody had to be behind a counter somewhere in the store, but I heard no voice, no greeting. The employee was probably at the other end. Couldn't even see us.

The world had forsaken me. Left me with this monster.

"We're going to make a call," the monster said. He guided me around the corner of the building to a pay phone.

My heart clutched. "To my parents? They'll pay. Anything you ask. Just ... please let me talk to them."

He chuckled low in his throat, an amused, evil laugh. "You think I stole you for *money*?"

10

B rittany checked her watch. Nine o'clock. Five hours had passed. She was in the great room with Rayne and Gary, who alternately sat and paced. The waiting was beyond endurance. Rayne kept saying she should be out there, doing *something* to help bring Shaley home. Brittany felt the same. Any little task would be better than this. But Al Scarrow had made it clear: they had many professionals working on the case. Rayne and Gary's job right now was to stay by their phones.

The cell phones sat on a nearby table, still silent and mocking. Brittany glared at Rayne's, willing it to ring.

Where was Shaley? Was she *alive*?

Brittany yanked that last thought from her head. Of course Shaley was alive. She had to be. Brittany could feel it. Her best friend was out there, somewhere. Brittany would know if Shaley were dead. Her heart would know. It would stop beating.

Everyone in the band had been questioned by detectives from the sheriff's department. Right now Kim and Morrey and the rest were scattered here and there around the mansion. But Brittany wouldn't leave Rayne's side. Rayne needed her. They needed each other, or they'd never survive this. And Rayne wasn't the only one that needed Brittany. A little while ago, she'd talked to Mick — for the third time — assuring him this wasn't his fault. All three bodyguards, Mick and Wendell and Lee, felt terrible. Each one blamed himself.

Mick's tanned face had looked ghostlike when Brittany and Rayne first talked to him together after Shaley's disappearance. He could hardly look Rayne in the eye. His own glazed with tears. Brittany had never seen him or any of Rayne's bodyguards cry. They were all men of steel.

"I'm sorry. I'm so ... sorry." Mick's voice caught.

"It's not your fault," Rayne said.

"It *is*. We—I was right there. Right out front. I *saw* that van go by toward the gate ..."

"So did Wendell," Rayne whispered. "And he's already told me *he's* to blame. Then Lee thinks *he* should somehow have known—and he was stationed in the house." Rayne shook her head. "None of us could have known. If we had, any one of us would have given our lives to save her."

Mick raised his eyes to hers. A tear stood in each corner. "I would have. I would."

"I know."

Now Brittany gazed at Rayne hunched in a chair and shuddered at the new revelation swirling in her head. An hour ago they'd received terrible news. Sheriff's deputies had found blood in the van.

Brittany's mind recited the fact again and again. *Blood in the van ... blood in the van ...*

When Rayne heard the news an hour ago, she'd thrown up.

It had only been a few drops of blood. But enough to tell them the story. Brittany's closest friend in the world had been hit. Hurt. Those drops on the driveway *had* been Shaley's blood. She'd been thrown in the back of that van bleeding. The imaginings and pictures crammed into Brittany's head until she thought her brain would burst open.

She couldn't *stand* this. Every minute, every breath seemed like her last. Her body wanted to block everything out. Shut down.

But she couldn't let herself fall apart. Shaley needed her. Somehow Brittany, Rayne, and Gary would bring Shaley home.

Agent Scarrow strode into the great room, carrying a sheet of paper, Ed Schering beside him. Ed was still in his tux, his silver-white hair no longer so perfectly combed. He'd been yelling at anybody and everybody, trying to fix things. Agent Scarrow had tried to calm him down. This wasn't a movie set. He wasn't bossing around actors and cameramen.

Ed veered off toward the kitchen.

Rayne pushed to her feet and faced Agent Scarrow. Brittany stood close by, bracing herself for what might come next. Her nerves tingled, her heart thumping against her ribs. "What's going on?" Gary pulled up beside Rayne.

Agent Scarrow handed Rayne the paper — a rough composite drawing of the kidnapper. "It's not the greatest, unfortunately. The security guard didn't get all that good a look at him."

Brittany and Gary leaned in, all three staring at the drawing. The man had a mean, fat face with hanging jowls and small eyes half hidden under a blue baseball cap with *San Diego* written across the front. He looked disgusting. And terrifying. But at least now they had a picture, something to go on.

What was he doing to Shaley right now?

There was something familiar about him ...

"Ever seen him before?" Agent Scarrow asked.

"I don't think so," Rayne said. "But ... I don't know."

Gary shook his head. "I've never seen him."

Brittany swallowed. "I think I have."

"Where?" Rayne's eyes rounded.

"I don't know." Brittany focused on the drawing and tried to remember. But the answer wouldn't come. Was she wrong about this? "I just ... I'm not sure. I'll keep thinking."

Agent Scarrow nodded. "You let me know if anything comes to you."

"Can I keep the drawing?" Brittany could hardly stand to look at the man's face again. But she had to. She had to figure out if she knew him from somewhere.

"Sure."

Rayne shoved the piece of paper into Brittany's hands as if she couldn't stand to touch it anymore.

Agent Scarrow pulled up one of the white wooden chairs rented for the wedding and gestured to Rayne and Gary. "Want to sit down? I need to tell you what we're doing with the van evidence."

Rayne lowered herself into her chair, sitting on the edge. Gary did the same. Brittany folded up the drawing and slid it into her jeans pocket. She'd study it later. Now she pulled up a chair and sat as well. She wanted to hear anything and everything the FBI agent had to say. Agent Scarrow sat down, legs apart.

"What about that drawing?" Rayne asked the agent.

"It's being disseminated. Law enforcement in all nearby states will be on the lookout. I wish it were a better picture. The hat keeps us from seeing his hair or the shape of his head. But it's something." Agent Scarrow leaned toward them, hands clasped and forearms on his legs. "The van is still being processed. Technicians are going through every square inch of it, searching for evidence. They've lifted fingerprints and taken samples of the blood. These samples can be sent to a local lab for a quick test to determine if the blood is human. If it is, the techs can then pretty quickly tell the blood type. Typing will give us a fair indication if it's Shaley's."

Rayne nodded. Brittany couldn't speak. She knew it was Shaley's. She *knew*.

Agent Scarrow gestured toward the upper level of the mansion. "You know a tech collected some hair from Shaley's brush in the bathroom so we can check DNA. If the blood type matches Shaley's, we'll need to run DNA tests to be sure it's hers. Those results take weeks. The other possibility, if the blood type *doesn't* match Shaley's, is that it might have come from the suspect. Maybe she scratched him and drew blood. If we get lucky and discover that we may have a sample of the suspect's blood, we can run DNA tests on the samples, then run the results through CODIS, the national DNA databank. If our suspect has been convicted of a felony, he'll be in the system. Or, if he's even been so much as arrested for a felony in California since the beginning of 2009, he'll be in the system. We've also extracted some hair samples from the driver's seat. These could belong to our suspect or to the original driver of the van. We obtained hair from the original driver. Technicians will examine the hairs to see if he can be excluded."

"Shaley and I were fingerprinted in school a few years ago." Brittany turned to Rayne. "Remember? It was voluntary. You signed her up."

"That's right, I did."

"Good to hear that." Agent Scarrow nodded. "We'll be able to check them against prints in the van. We'll also run any finger-prints lifted, especially those from the driver's area, through the California database. If the suspect has been arrested within this state, he'll be in there. If we don't find a match there, we'll widen our search to western states, then the whole country."

Gary leaned forward and ran his hands up and down his face. Then heaved back in his chair. "All this is fine, but this is *evidence*. We don't want evidence. We just want Shaley back."

"I under—"

"No, you don't understand!" Sudden anger seized his face. "You *can't* understand! We just need her found. And now we don't even know what car they're in!"

Rayne squeezed Gary's arm—hard. He was usually so calm, and Brittany knew Rayne needed him to stay that way. Right now everything he said and did seemed to flow into her.

Agent Scarrow looked down at the marble floor and cleared his throat. "Mr. Donovon, I do know what it's like to have a child snatched away. It happened to my own daughter fourteen years ago. She was three."

Rayne's mouth sagged open. She and Gary both spoke at once.

"I'm so sorry—"

"We didn't know—"

"It's okay." Agent Scarrow held up his palm. He had long fin-gers. "We're not here to talk about that. We're here to find your daughter. I just want you to know I'm going to do everything I can to find Shaley. I will give this case everything I've got."

Rayne surveyed him, as if afraid to ask the same question that hung in Brittany's mind. "What happened to your daughter?"

Agent Scarrow swiveled his head to look through the rear wall of glass out to the back gardens. Regret pinched his face. Brittany knew before he spoke what his answer would be.

"Her body was found four days later."

"Oh." Brittany closed her eyes. Grief and fear surged through her. Agent Scarrow's daughter would now have been seventeen, her and Shaley's age.

"I'm so sorry," Rayne whispered.

Gary shook his head. "I'm doubly sorry. I should never have ... "

For a moment silence hung in the air. Brittany stared at the huge bouquets of coral and white flowers near the wall of glass — where the wedding party would have stood for the ceremony. The FBI agent's words chilled her to the bone. They would *not* find Shaley's body four days from now. They wouldn't. No way could they live without Shaley.

Agent Scarrow smiled grimly. "I shouldn't have brought it up. Every case is different. I don't want you to think this one has to end like that. But I do want to say that's what got me into law enforcement. After that I wanted nothing more than to get bad guys off the streets." He stood up. "For me — this case, bringing Shaley home? It's personal."

11

At the grungy pay phone, Monster Man crowded next to me. He smelled sweaty and his breath stank. The phone hung from the wall of the gas station. At least we weren't in the tight quarters of a phone booth.

The man's last words echoed in my head. *"You think I stole you for money?"* What did that mean? Why did he laugh?

"Keep your head down," he ordered.

He still didn't want me to get a good look at his face. Hope knocked around inside me. He didn't want me to be able to identify him later. Which meant he planned to let me go.

"You're going to call your mom."

Yes!

But I showed no emotion. I didn't dare let him see how much I wanted this—how much I *needed* to hear my mom's voice. If he knew what it meant to me, he might change his mind.

"I'll be listening. You're going to tell her only what I tell you to say. Got it?"

"Yes." My heart banged around in my chest. *Please, please.*

He put his beefy hand on the phone. "You say anything I don't tell you to say, I will make you very sorry."

"Okay."

"First, tell her you never wanted her to marry that lowlife."

Shock ran through me. My chin came up.

"Don't look at me!" He shoved me against the wall. My head

bounced off the brick. I gasped. Tucked my chin down low, trembling.

"Did you get that?" He squeezed my upper arm.

"Yes." My voice croaked. How could I say such a horrible thing to Mom? It was so *not true*.

"Then tell her this." He continued to talk, pouring out vile words that turned my limbs to ice.

Mom would never believe me. Never. She'd know I was being coached.

That realization pushed determination through my veins.

Fine. Let him tell me crazy things to say. The crazier they were, the more Mom would know he was making me say them. At least she'd hear my voice, and I'd hear hers. At least she'd know I was okay.

He lifted the receiver. "Punch in her number."

I raised my hand. Pressed the keys. Monster Man bent close and held the receiver between our heads.

Through the speaker "You Are My Always" started to play. One of my favorite Rayne songs. It was Mom's default ringback tone. Tears sprang to my eyes. I closed them and listened to Mom sing.

The music cut off. "Hello?"

Mom's voice pitched high, tight. *Mom, Mom!* I wanted to scream and cry. I wanted to be with her, fling myself into her arms.

For a drawn-out second, I couldn't even speak.

"Hello?"

"Hi, Mom."

"Shaley!" Her voice cracked. "Where are you, are you okay?"

Monster Man pinched the skin on the back of my arm. "Say it," he snarled in my ear.

No. I wanted to tell Mom how much I loved her and Gary. How I was going to get home to them, no matter what it took.

"*Say* it!"

My jaw hardened. "I ... Mom, I never wanted you to marry Gary. He's a lowlife." My voice sounded like someone else's. "For a long time,

I've been planning to run away just before the wedding. I don't ..."
My hands fisted. I squeezed my eyes shut. "I don't ever want to see
you again. Don't come looking for me because even if you found me,
I would never come home."

"Sha—"

Monster Man slapped down the metal hook and cut the call. I
leaned against the wall, sick to my stomach.

He hung up the receiver. "There now. That wasn't so hard,
was it?"

I stared at the asphalt. His scuffed brown shoes. My rolled-up
jeans bottoms and bare feet. I wanted to die.

"Let's go." He turned me around and pointed me toward the car.

From somewhere deep within me reason whispered. I raised
my eyes, took in the color of the SUV, the make. An old blue Ford
Explorer. License plate 2ZRY394. I stared at the plate, willing myself to remember it. After I got back home safe—somehow—those
letters and numbers could lead the police to this man. I wanted him
to *pay*.

He opened the Explorer's back door. *2ZRY* ... What were the
numbers? 9–4–6? No. 3–4–9. No.

They were gone from my head.

My whole body slumped. What did it matter? He was talking
like I'd never go back home.

"Get in back where you were." He pushed my shoulders.

My throat jerked in a swallow. "You didn't ask my mom for a
ransom."

He laughed that same derisive chuckle. "I told you I don't want
money, Shaley."

"Then what do you want?"

He laid his hand on the back of my neck. I cringed from his
touch. "I'm taking you to a cabin in Montana. I've done you a favor,
taking you away from your sinful lifestyle, Shaley. I'm going to teach
you spiritual truth. We'll start a community of people waiting for
Christ's return."

Was this guy some crazed cult leader? I felt even sicker. People disappeared into cults and never came out. "What do I have to do with your 'community'?"

He closed his fingers around my neck. "I've chosen *you* to be my wife."

12

Brittany clutched both hands to her chest, eyes fastened on the recording device. Its tiny speakers had projected Shaley's voice into the room just seconds ago. So real. So *alive*. Now — nothing.

"Shaley!" Rayne cried into her cell phone. "*Shaley!*"

Gary leaned toward Rayne, forehead creased and muscles looking stiff, as if he wanted to pull Shaley through the phone and into his arms. Kim, Morrey, Rich, Ross, and Stan huddled nearby, listening, waiting.

Agent Scarrow stood a few feet away, legs apart and arms crossed. His head tilted, his eyes fixed upon the recorder.

"Shaley!" Rayne's voice broke.

Please, God, please, Brittany begged. *Let us hear her again.*

Mocking silence.

Rayne lowered the phone. "She's gone."

"She didn't mean it!" Brittany's eyes filled with tears. "You know somebody made her say those things!"

Agent Scarrow whipped a small notepad and pen from his shirt pocket and reached for Rayne's cell phone. He checked the ID of the phone call and wrote down the number. Unclipped his own cell and punched in a number for auto dial. "We just got a call." He turned away. "From the number ... "

Weakness stole into Brittany's legs, and the agent's voice faded. Shaley was okay. She *was*.

Agent Scarrow continued speaking rapidly into his cell, then waited.

Rayne sank into the nearest wooden chair. She gripped her knees and stared at the floor. Brittany knelt beside her. "She didn't mean it."

"I know. I know."

"Brittany's right," Kim said. "Somebody made her say that."

"I know."

"But why?" Gary paced, hands pressed against his temples and elbows thrust out. His voice was ragged. "They didn't ask for money."

Brittany's wild relief at hearing her best friend's voice faded. What if whoever had taken Shaley didn't *want* money? What if he had no intention of letting her go?

Rayne sagged back against her chair. Gary fell into the seat beside her and pulled her close. Rayne clung to him and shook.

"We can't sit here any longer." The words burst from Brittany. "We have to *do* something."

Rayne pulled away from Gary's arms. "Brittany's right. We needed to hear from them first. Well, we've heard."

Gary nodded. "We should schedule a press conference in the morning. Make a public plea for the return of our daughter. And beg every person out there to be on the lookout for her. Someone's bound to see them."

Brittany glanced at Agent Scarrow, who was still talking on the phone. Sunday morning seemed eons away. It was only midnight now. She would not sleep. She could barely *breathe*.

"Right. Thanks." The agent clicked off the line and turned to Rayne and Gary. "The call came from a pay phone at a gas station just across the Nevada border."

Rayne's jaw slackened. "Nevada?"

Brittany stared at him. Where could the kidnapper be taking Shaley? *Why?*

"Our office is calling in local law enforcement right now," Agent Scarrow continued. "They'll take fingerprints from the phone, see if they match any lifted from the van. They'll also question employees at the station. If the place has working security cameras, the police can look at the tape." He rubbed his hands together, energy bristling from him. "This is good. Gives us something to work with. And most importantly, we know Shaley's alive."

PART 2
Sunday

13

For the millionth time, I checked the clock on the Explorer dashboard. Just past midnight. Not long after the gas station, we'd left the freeway to take smaller back roads. For all I knew, we were going in circles. It was clear my captor took those little highways to avoid being spotted on major roads. Finally we'd been forced to hit the freeway again.

Every minute seemed an eternity. Like time had stopped. My real life had stopped. My body felt numb. In my mind I tried to stay strong. Tried to figure out ... something.

I sat in the front passenger seat, not because I wanted to be anywhere near Monster Man, but because he told me to. He wanted me near him for company. I was supposed to help keep him awake so we wouldn't crash. But I wasn't allowed to turn my head and look at him.

What did I care if we crashed? I'd rather die than live in some wilderness Montana cabin with this man. But I clung to one thought: I *had* to get back to Mom and Dad. And Brittany, and the band. I had to win my *life* back.

We'd driven through the bottom tip of Nevada and into Arizona. We must have just hit a corner of Arizona, because not too much later I saw the state sign for Utah.

Utah. Three states away from home.

My feet were cold. I needed shoes. I rubbed one foot on top of the other. The rest of my body still ached and would hurt for days. I wasn't in any shape to make a run for it if we stopped. Not at all. It wasn't my strength that would get me out of this. It was my brain. I had to outwit Monster Man. And I had to fight back the panic that clawed at my throat every other minute.

I focused out my window. The freeway looked desolate, few cars besides ours. Even so, my kidnapper didn't drive over the speed limit. Wouldn't do to be pulled over by a cop.

"You're supposed to be talking to me." He hunched over the wheel, frowning at the road. Tiredness pulled at his mouth, his eyes. But a steely, dogged determination wafted from him, as if he were on a mission. As if he were *right* to kidnap me.

I'm going to teach you spiritual truth, he'd said. The words chilled me. This man was deluded.

How do you rationalize with someone who's insane?

"Talk!" he snapped.

I jumped. My gaze shifted to his ugly profile. Would he hit me for looking at him?

Strength, Shaley. Play along. Learn things you can use against him.

I folded my arms and shivered. "So what's your name?" My voice sounded dull, hopeless.

"Joshua."

Joshua. A biblical name. Was it his real one?

"Where are we going in Montana?"

"To the cabin I built for us."

"But where in Montana? That's a big state."

"Up near the Canadian border."

Ice flowed through my veins. What if he took me *into* Canada? How would anyone ever find us then?

"Tell me about this community you want to start." I forced the name onto my tongue. "Joshua."

He scowled at the road. "This country is falling into evil. Drugs, sex. People killing each other." He threw me a disgusted look. "Rock music."

My fingers curled into my palms until the nails bit into skin. How *dare* he sneer at my mom and dad, and the members of Rayne. Not one of them would ever *think* of doing what he'd done to me.

My anger felt good. Gave me courage.

"What's wrong with rock music?"

"It's full of sin and degradation. Bunch a loud noise and violent lyrics —"

"Rayne's lyrics are never violent."

"Full of sex —"

"They're not full of that either."

He turned his head and glared demon eyes at me. Inside I recoiled, but I forced myself to stare back at him. *You want to hit me, fine. But don't you talk about my parents.*

"There's still a lot of sass in you." His tongue poked beneath his upper lip. He turned back to view the road. "No matter." He said the words almost to himself. Low. Menacing. "I'll rid you of it soon enough."

Fresh panic spun through me. What would he do to me?

For a wild moment I wanted to be back in the trunk of a car. At least there I wasn't near him. At least there I could fight, scream when I wanted to scream. Now every emotion had to be pushed down deep inside me. Because I knew if I let it out now, I'd never get it back in. I'd attack him right here, driving or not. Hit and slap and scratch his eyes out.

Sweat slicked the back of my T-shirt. I clenched my jaw, breathed in, breathed out. I could *not* lose it here. I had to stay one step ahead of him.

I swallowed hard. "I asked you about the community. What's it going to be like?"

"It'll be people who want to serve God the right way. Women dressed modestly. Everyone in church every day."

"What church?"

He made a sound in his throat, as if I'd asked a stupid question. "*My* church."

"You're a pastor?"

"I'm a prophet."

Joshua the prophet. Oh, yeah, this guy's head was on straight.

I was trapped by a madman.

"How will we live?"

"Off the land. We'll farm, raise cattle. Sell our goods to people in town."

The last word made my heart leap. "What town?"

"You'll know soon enough."

"How far away from the cabin is it?"

He smiled. It was the most evil expression I'd ever seen. "Far enough that you can't run to it."

Just watch me. He had *no* idea what I'd do to get back to my family.

I gazed at the freeway eaten up by the Explorer's wheels. Every mile took me farther away.

I could see fine out of my right eye. But my left had only half the vision. Cautiously I touched the area with my fingertips. It still felt swollen. Tender.

My hand slid away. Woodenly, I stared out the windshield. The world looked black and vast. Like it would swallow me whole.

"You know how to sew?" Joshua asked.

"No."

He grunted. "You'll learn."

I'd never threaded a needle in my life.

My thoughts turned to Mom. What was she doing right now? She wouldn't be sleeping. She had to be going crazy with worry. Dad too. Had they stayed at Ed Schering's mansion? Did anyone have any idea what had happened to me?

Be strong, Mom and Dad. If you are, I will be too.

14

Nearly three o'clock in the morning. I'd been kidnapped eleven hours ago. *Eleven hours.* It seemed like forever.

I still couldn't believe this was real.

In the front passenger seat, I shifted uncomfortably. My body felt cramped and torn. I needed to go to the bathroom again.

The freeway stretched on and on, never ending.

Fifteen minutes later I saw a sign for a highway exit. Joshua slowed and turned off the freeway.

I tensed. "Where are we going?"

"Takin' a back road to a cabin."

Every muscle stilled. Driving had been bad enough. But stopping ... "Why?"

"I got to get some rest."

Was he telling the truth?

"Whose cabin is it?"

"A friend of mine."

No, not *two* men. "Does he know we're coming?"

"Sure. But he's already in Montana, waiting for us. He left the electricity on so we could use the place."

"You mean he's someone in your community?"

"Yeah. Me and him are like brothers."

Could a monster like this care for someone like a brother?

Suddenly the word *us* registered. I turned my head to stare at Joshua's jowly profile. "You mean he knows you're bringing *me*?"

Joshua snickered. "He knows I'm bringing a wife."

But did he know Joshua had *kidnapped* me?

My mind churned. I stared out my side window, thinking. Maybe some neighbor near his friend's cabin would see us. Maybe they'd recognize my face. Surely my kidnapping had been on the news by now.

Joshua smirked, as if he knew what I was thinking. "No neighbors around to bother us. Besides, in this area people mind their own business."

My chin lowered. I stared at my lap.

Why, God?

It didn't make any sense. In the last year, I, then Mom and Dad, had become Christians. We were trying to live right. Why would God let this happen? And worst of all, Joshua was doing this in *God's* name.

A lightning bolt ought to burst out of heaven and strike him dead.

We hit the end of the exit. Joshua turned right onto a two-lane highway. Full blackness descended, not one other car in sight. The Explorer's headlights cut through the thick dark like swords. We might as well have been on Mars.

Never had I felt so isolated.

And what would happen when we reached the cabin? When Joshua didn't have to drive?

I pulled my arms against my sides and tried to breathe.

"We'll be there soon," Joshua said.

Terror kicked around inside me. My eyes squeezed shut. I focused on the lull of the car, wishing for sleep. Telling myself this wasn't real.

After some time the Explorer slowed. My head jerked up. Joshua turned left, and our tires popped over gravel. Trees lined the road on either side. Then a clearing. Our headlights washed over a two-story log cabin surrounded by weedy grass. A simple detached garage. Joshua pulled up next to the garage. "Stay here."

He slid out of the Explorer, leaned down, and pulled up the garage door. It rolled open with a grating sound. Joshua returned to the SUV and drove inside. He cut the engine. "Let's go."

The garage fell into darkness. Not even a window in the place to let moonlight through.

I couldn't move.

He opened his door and glared at me, a message to obey. The overhead light in the Explorer had flicked on, washing down over his face. I stared back. In an instant I took in the beady brown eyes and round, pudgy face. Fat lips. A buzz cut.

My brain flashed on pictures I'd seen of that face. The memory jolted me.

No, no.

Dear God, don't let it be him.

15

Three thirty in the morning, Rayne and Gary were on their knees in the mansion's library. Rayne's legs were going to sleep, but she hardly noticed. She couldn't rest. Couldn't do anything right now to help find Shaley. But she and Gary could pray.

Brittany and the rest of the band members were in their bedrooms, giving Gary and Rayne some time by themselves. Not one of them had wanted to leave Rayne's side. She knew they weren't sleeping. Ed Schering had hugged Rayne a short time ago, before straggling upstairs to his suite. Al was on the phone in the TV room. The man never stopped. He was either on a call or taking notes or conferring with the local sheriff's deputies who'd come in and out every hour.

"God, please help us find her. *Soon.*" Gary's voice sounded raw and cracked. He pressed close to Rayne, one arm around her back. He'd broken down and cried more than once as they prayed. "Be with us during our press conference. Let someone who sees it on the news lead us to Shaley."

The press conference was scheduled for ten o'clock in the morning. Rayne and Gary were putting up a one-hundred-thousand-dollar reward for Shaley's safe return. They both would make a statement. Al would handle the rest, giving out information and taking questions from reporters.

Gary rubbed Rayne's shoulder. "And help Rayne —"

Footsteps sounded, and the door opened. Rayne looked up to see Al at the entrance. He carried a notebook-size folder. He raised both hands. "Didn't mean to disturb you. We have some new information."

Violent fear and hope shot through Rayne. She struggled to her feet, Gary helping her up.

"What's happened?" Gary demanded.

Al came into the room and gestured toward the rich chocolate leather couch. "You want to sit down?"

Rayne walked around the large glass coffee table to perch on the end of the couch, Gary at her side. Her muscles felt tied in knots.

Al sat in an armchair and angled around to face them. His eyes looked tired, but his shoulders were as straight as they'd been since he first arrived. Rayne felt a spray of jealousy. If only she were merely tired instead of weighted with a thousand pounds of fear. Her head throbbed even after two aspirin, and her mind still reeled.

But Al had been through this once. He *knew* how it felt. And his daughter hadn't come home.

The jealousy spritzed away.

Al opened the folder and withdrew a sheet of paper. "Couple things. First, we did match fingerprints in the back of the van to Shaley. The blood drops are human and her type. And the hair is consistent with Shaley's hair."

Rayne's throat constricted. She managed a tight nod.

"Also, we were able to match other fingerprints from the van to one lifted from the pay phone in Nevada. For that reason, and another one I'll tell you in a minute, we're certain this is our man. We ran those prints through the California database and got a hit." Al handed the paper to Rayne. "His name is Ronald Fledger. Recognize that?"

Ronald Fledger? Rayne snapped her eyes down to stare at the paper. A mug shot — one she'd seen before. Sickness whirled in her stomach. She shoved the picture into Gary's hands. "He was stalking Shaley a couple of years ago. Kept sending her pictures and letters, saying how she needed to be with him, and he was going to make sure that happened. He really scared us. Sounded like a nut case, no telling what he might do. We turned all the evidence over to the police. They arrested him. I thought he was in jail ... "

"He got out a few months ago." Al was watching Gary. "Ever see him before?"

Gary's face had paled. He shook his head. "But I've heard the story of what he sent to Shaley."

Rayne and Gary locked eyes in a long, horrified look.

That crazy man had her daughter. Rayne's hands started to shake. No. *No.* "His hair was so much longer then." The words sandpapered her throat. "I didn't recognize the composite you showed me earlier."

"He does look different with shorter hair." Al continued to focus on Gary.

Gary dropped the mug shot onto the glass table as if it were a snake. He licked his lips. "At least ... we know who to look for."

"Yes." Al picked up the paper and returned it to his folder. "This is already being disseminated." He cleared his throat. "Now — the second reason we know this is our man. Nevada police interviewed the employee on duty at the gas station during the time of Shaley's call. Unfortunately the employee's not much help. He said people come in and out, and he's often reading a magazine. He doesn't tend to notice faces unless someone comes up to the checkout counter."

Reading a magazine? What kind of employee was he?

"But the deputies pulled the tape from the security camera at the station and took it back to their department. It's not the best of tapes in that it doesn't constantly run the time across the bottom. So they had to watch it a while until they could approximate the time of Shaley's call — "

"Did they *see* her?" Rayne leaned forward. *Please, please.*

"Yes."

"Oh." Rayne's right hand pressed to her mouth.

Gary gripped Rayne's arm. "What did she look like? Was she okay?"

Al flexed his shoulders. "It was definitely Shaley, although it's not a close-up of her face. In fact she kept her head down the whole time. And the tape is somewhat grainy. She's no longer wearing the bridesmaid dress — she's now in jeans and a plain white T-shirt. Her hair was stuck up under a blue baseball cap. When they enlarged the shot they could see *San Diego* on the front of the cap. It's the same one shown in our composite of the suspect. *That's* why we're sure we have our man."

For a moment no one spoke. Rayne tried to absorb the information, but her brain couldn't focus.

"He had clothes for her." Gary's tone had a raw edge. "He planned this so ... he planned everything."

"She'd stand out too much in the dress." Rayne's tongue seemed to move all by itself. Her mind was on Shaley. How *was* she? Was she hurt? Hungry? She had to be terrified.

She kept her head down the whole time. That wasn't Shaley. He'd forced her to do that. Or she'd been so scared she couldn't even hold her head up.

Dread coated Rayne. She opened her mouth but only a moan escaped. Tears sprang to her eyes. She sagged against Gary. "Oh, God, please. I just can't ..."

Gary slid his arm around her. "I know," he whispered in her ear. "But this is good news. We know what she's wearing."

Rayne fought to control herself. Slowly she pulled away from Gary, forced her chin up.

"There's more." Al tapped his folder. "The tape picked up their vehicle and license plate. They're traveling in a 1997 blue Ford Explorer. We ran the plate and discovered the vehicle was stolen from the Santa Barbara area two days ago."

"Two days?" Gary rubbed his jaw. "More planning."

Rayne pushed a strand of hair from her face. While they'd happily counted the hours until the wedding, this man, this *beast*, had been planning his horrible act.

"But how did he know my ring would be brought in that van?" Gary's eyes remained on Al. "Those plans weren't in place until *after* he stole the Explorer."

Al spread his hands. "That we don't know."

Rayne found her tongue. "You'll give out the information about the car and license plate number at the press conference, right? And show the mug shot? Then everyone can be looking for this man."

Al tilted his head. "We're ... discussing that."

"What's to discuss?" Rayne's voice turned sharp. "And isn't what's said at the conference our decision?"

"Not entirely." Al leaned forward. "Look. I and the others working on this case don't know which direction will be the safest for Shaley. If we tell the public, true, they can help us look for the vehicle. Without the public's help, it could take us far longer to find Shaley, and every minute counts. On the other hand, we have to think from the suspect's point of view. He doesn't know *we* know what vehicle they're in, or that we know who he is. But if that information is disseminated to the media, he could turn on any radio or TV and hear it. That could make him very angry. What if he takes his anger out on Shaley?"

Oh.

Rayne looked at Gary. His expression was dazed — the same way she felt. The FBI agent was right — either choice could lead to terrible consequences.

"What should we do?" she whispered.

Gary closed his eyes. "I don't know. I just ... don't know."

A rock fell through Rayne's stomach. How to know what to do? How? *God, please tell us.* Rayne searched Gary's face and knew he was thinking the same terrible thought.

What if they made the wrong choice — and Shaley paid for it with her life?

16

The pebbles in the driveway hurt my bare feet. I hobbled over them toward the cabin, Joshua grasping my elbow.

A half moon and bright stars lit our way. If I'd been out with friends in a rural place like this, away from the lights of the city, I'd have been amazed at the starry sky. You couldn't see such a thing in Southern California. But now the night mocked me. How could the sky hang with such beauty when my world had turned so black and terrifying?

Two steps led up to the porch. Joshua still held on to me as we climbed them.

He pulled a key from his pants pocket and unlocked the door to the cabin. I cowered beside him, trapped and trembling. I couldn't go inside with this man. I *couldn't*. This man—this *prophet of God*—was the man who'd stalked me two years ago. Who'd insisted I'd one day be his. That man had been arrested and sent to prison. But now here he was, leading me into a dark cabin in the middle of nowhere.

Panic clawed at my throat. I shoved it back down. *Please, God, protect me. Show me what to do.*

"Wh-what are we going to do here?" My voice shook. My cheek and left eye hurt, as did my arms and hands. Joshua's grip radiated pain through my elbow.

No answer. He put the key back in his pocket and opened the door. Its hinges creaked. Still holding my arm, Joshua leaned around and fumbled at the wall with his other hand. Light flicked on inside.

"Come on." He pushed me over the threshold first, then closed and locked the door behind us.

The smell hit me. Oppressive and musty.

We stood in a denlike room with an old brown couch and a pea-green armchair. A wooden table with books and a few scattered magazines. Opposite the couch sat a small TV on a black stand. Farther to the left, the room flowed into a small kitchen. Even from where I stood, I could see burn marks on the short counter space. The stove was off-white and battered. A small refrigerator. A table for two people. Everywhere I looked I saw dust and grime, and what looked like white dog hair.

My ankles trembled.

To our right rose a wooden staircase. Any bedrooms and the bathroom must be upstairs.

I tore my gaze from the stairs and turned back toward the kitchen. My eyes landed on a small black object on the counter.

Telephone.

My heart skipped. Was it connected?

Joshua headed for the kitchen. "There's some food in the refrigerator. Want a sandwich?"

Like I could eat.

"No. Thanks."

I watched him turn on the overhead light in the kitchen. It was a bare bulb and bright. He opened the refrigerator door and checked inside. Everything in me wanted to bolt out of that cabin, make a run for it. But where would I go? And how far would I get in bare feet before he caught me? It would make him so *mad*.

"Come on, Shaley, don't stand there looking so stupid."

I'm not stupid.

The defensive thought blossomed into an idea. Maybe I should play stupid. Or at least so scared I didn't have any fight left in me. Let him think he'd beaten me down, that I just wanted to get along with him. Maybe then he'd get sloppy, not watch me every minute. Somehow I'd get to the phone . . .

If it even worked.

I forced myself to walk through the den. Around the brown couch and closer to the kitchen. My bare feet felt every piece of dirt on the wooden floor. Little piles of white hair gathered along the wall.

"Your friend have a dog?"

"Yeah." Joshua was pulling cheese, lunch meat, and bread from the refrigerator. "Little white terrier."

"What's his name?" I stopped near the green armchair, about four feet from the kitchen's threshold. I could see a clock on the wall. It read past four o'clock. We'd changed time zones.

"Jack."

A shiver ran through me. I rubbed my arms. "What's your friend's name?"

"Caleb."

Caleb. I should have guessed.

"Like in the Bible." I tried to keep the disgust from my voice. This man was such a lying hypocrite. "Joshua and Caleb. Out to settle the Promised Land."

Joshua looked around at me, eyebrows raised. "You know about that?"

"I read the Bible too, you know."

He gave me a steely look. "Wouldn't have expected that."

"There's a lot you don't know about me. Or my parents."

Who are surely moving heaven and earth to look for me right now.

Joshua jerked upright to face me, mouth twisting. "You better watch your mouth."

I melted back, heart rat-ratting. How could he change so fast? "Sorry. I just meant . . . we have a lot to learn about each other."

Joshua pierced me with a long gaze. Then he grunted and turned around to make his sandwich.

Movement on the floor caught my eye. A small gray mouse. I watched as he scuttled into the kitchen, past Joshua's foot, and under the refrigerator. My shoulders drew in.

"I need to go to the bathroom."

"Upstairs."

I turned and surveyed the steps. I didn't want to go up there, near the bedrooms. What if Joshua came behind and trapped me?

But it had been hours since I'd used the toilet.

With a furtive glance at Joshua, I turned to walk back through the den.

I'd expected the stairs to creak, like the front door. They didn't. My bruised hand slid along the pole railing.

At the top of the steps, I turned left into a hall that ran the width of the cabin. Three open doors stood on my left. I peeked in the first and saw a small room with a single bed and a three-drawer dresser. One window overlooked the front, with torn gray curtains.

The second door led to the bathroom. I slipped inside and locked myself in. I headed to the small mirror above the sink. Dared to look at my reflection.

Air swirled in my throat. I hung on to the sink, gazing into the face I didn't know. It was even worse than before. My left eye was black and swollen half shut. The bruising ran clear to my jaw. My eye makeup was even more smeared, one dark line tracing down my right cheek.

I turned on the water. It flowed out a light brown. I let it run until it looked clear, then carefully splashed my face — at least the right side. The left side felt too tender to wash. One towel hung from a rack on the wall. I considered it, then pulled it off. Smelled it and wrinkled my nose. Replacing it, I reached for toilet paper to wipe the makeup smear from my face.

In the medicine cabinet I found an old rubber band. Who knew why it was there. I used it to pull my ratty hair into a loose ponytail.

When I finished in the bathroom, I ventured into the hall. Leaning forward, I listened, head cocked toward the stairs. The sound of shuffling feet drifted to me, and the closing of a cabinet.

I looked in the direction of the third door. What was in there?

Creeping farther down the hall, I peeked inside. A second bedroom, bigger than the first. With a double bed. My breath shuddered. I didn't want Joshua to come up and catch me anywhere near that thing.

As I turned to leave I saw a telephone on the nightstand.

My body froze. I stared at the phone, feeling the rise and fall of my chest with each breath. Could I walk across the room and pick it up without Joshua hearing?

What if the floor creaked? I'd be right above the kitchen. He might guess what I was doing. If he'd turned so angry just a minute ago over nothing ...

I swallowed, eyes riveted to the phone. Then leaned back toward the stairs, listening.

No sound of footfalls on the wooden steps.

Swiveling, I hurried across the bedroom floor, taking long, low strides. Trying not to make even the tiniest noise. For the first time I was glad I was barefoot. In seven steps I stood at the nightstand, hand hovering over the receiver.

What if it *did* work, and he was on the downstairs phone?

My fingers grazed the black plastic. I bit my lip, glanced back at the door.

Carefully, I eased up the receiver.

I lifted it to my ear — and heard a dial tone.

Relief weakened my knees. I jabbed a finger at the first digit to dial 9-1-1.

"Shaley?" Joshua bellowed from below me.

I jumped, every inch of me tingling. Quickly, but with no sound, I replaced the receiver.

"What you doing up there, girl?"

Footsteps sounded on the main-level floor.

In seconds I crossed the bedroom and into the hall.

From the stairwell drifted the sound of Joshua's foot on the bottom step.

I hurried noiselessly until I was even with the bathroom. Joshua continued climbing, his steps heavy and lumbering.

At the threshold of the bathroom I stopped, gulped in air. "I'm here."

Joshua appeared at the top stair and turned toward me. "What's taking you so long?" Suspicion darkened his face.

I pressed against the doorway. "Just looking at myself in the mirror."

He grunted.

Something within me stirred, giving me courage. I folded my arms. "You said I was going to be your wife."

He snorted. "Not *was*. *Will*."

I stared at him evenly. "Is *this* the way you want your wife to look?" One hand gestured toward my face.

Joshua considered me as if for the first time. He tilted his head and shrugged. "The bruises won't last."

"They will if you keep hitting me."

"I won't hit you if you do what I say."

"I *am* doing what you say."

He gave me a twisted grin. "Then there's no need to worry, is there?"

We eyed each other.

"*Is* there?" He walked toward me.

"No."

"That's good." He stopped four feet away. "Now if you'd kindly step out of my way, I'd like to use the bathroom." His tone was mocking.

I moved aside.

Joshua shot me a hard look, stepped into the bathroom, and shut the door.

This was my chance — however short.

I turned and scurried on cat feet toward the phone.

17

Four in the morning. Shaley had been missing for twelve hours. Brittany's eyes felt gritty as she paced the library. Gary sat on the edge of the couch, head down, hands clasped between his legs. Rayne was beside him.

Brittany's nerves were brittle. Rayne and Gary had told her about the conversation they'd had with Agent Scarrow. *Ronald Fledger.* Brittany shook her head. She should have remembered him. She *knew* the suspect composite looked familiar. To think Shaley was with that awful man. It was just too horrible.

And now Rayne and Gary didn't know what to do — tell the public the information they knew, or not? Even when they decided, Agent Scarrow had said the FBI may not agree.

"Tell them," Brittany had declared. "Who cares what the FBI says? Anything to help find Shaley — we have to do it."

That was ten minutes ago. No one had spoken since.

"I agree we should tell the media what car she's in." Gary's words were aimed at the floor. He sounded broken and exhausted. "With everybody looking ..."

"I think so too," Rayne said, "but they — "

Agent Scarrow entered the room, carrying the tape recorder used during all his interviews. Rayne narrowed her eyes at it.

Now what? Brittany sighed. The FBI were supposed to be the experts here. But Shaley was Rayne and Gary's daughter. Shouldn't *they* have the final say in what information was included in the press conference?

"I'd like to talk to you, Gary." The agent gave him a polite smile.

Brittany's antennae went up. Something wasn't right here.

"Why?" Rayne asked. "You've interviewed him already."

"Something's come up." Agent Scarrow gestured toward the door. "You want to go somewhere else to talk? Maybe the dining room?"

Gary stared at him blankly. "I don't care. We can do it right here."

"Maybe we should talk alone."

"Why?" Rayne demanded. "What's going on?"

Gary shook his head. "I want Rayne here. Brittany can stay too."

Agent Scarrow looked from him to Rayne to Brittany, as if making a decision. "Okay." He set the recorder on the glass coffee table in front of the couch and turned it on. "You want to sit down, Brittany?"

"I'm fine."

Agent Scarrow took the armchair and swiveled around to face Gary. "Four a.m. Sunday." He spoke toward the tape recorder. "Interview with Gary Donovon. Rayne and Brittany are also present." He looked to Gary. "I've listened to the tape from Shaley's call over and over. One thing that bothers me is this statement: 'I never wanted you to marry Gary. He's a lowlife.'"

Brittany folded her arms. Why was he even repeating those awful words?

"You know she didn't mean that," Rayne said.

The agent cleared his throat. "That's just it — Ronald Fledger made her say it." He turned to Gary. "But why that term — *lowlife*? It makes me think the kidnapper knows your background."

"What does Gary's past have to do with this?" Rayne retorted.

Gary shrugged. "Who *doesn't* know? Once Rayne and I got back together, it was all over the tabloids."

It sure was. Plus a lot of lies. Gary's conviction for armed robbery, his years in prison. The former cell mate he'd asked to get close to Shaley upon his release from prison so the man could feed Gary information about the daughter he'd never met. How the tabloids had twisted *that* story.

"True." Agent Scarrow nodded. "Still I wonder why, of all things he apparently told Shaley to say, he included that."

Gary frowned at him. "What are you getting at?"

Agent Scarrow tilted his head. "Do you think Ronald Fledger has any ties to anyone you knew in prison?"

Rayne made a face. "That would be quite a coincidence."

"I've told you everything I know." Gary spread his hands. "I can't think of anyone in prison who had it in for me. Who might set Fledger up to do this for some kind of revenge. Besides, I was in a Nevada prison, and Fledger was in California. But if someone was paroled and got this crazy idea ..."

"Do you have contact with anyone who was in prison with you, or may now be out?"

"I told you in our first interview — no."

"You're sure about that."

"I'm positive."

"What *is* this?" Rayne demanded.

"Let's talk about your ring." Al stayed focused on Gary.

Rayne huffed. "You've already talked about *that* too!"

"Rayne, be *quiet*." Gary frowned at her, then looked back to the FBI agent. "What about the ring?"

"You told me it was the wrong size, which surprised you. So you made last-minute plans to have it resized here in Santa Barbara and delivered to you."

"Right."

"But the question remains — how did the suspect know that van was coming here, and that Shaley would be personally meeting it to get the ring?"

"I don't *know*."

"Shaley told the jeweler she'd be meeting the van," Brittany interjected. The agent gave her a look, but she wasn't about to keep out of this. "You should be asking Pogh Jewelers these questions. *Those* people are the only ones outside the wedding party who knew that."

Agent Scarrow looked at Gary—and Gary stared back. Suddenly Brittany understood. She and Rayne exchanged a horrified, knowing glance.

"Are you saying you think *Gary* is involved in this?" Rayne sounded shocked.

The FBI agent lifted a hand. "It's a base I have to cover."

"*What?*" Gary straightened.

Rayne eyed Agent Scarrow, open-mouthed. "No, you don't. You certainly don't! Because Gary didn't have a *thing* to do with this! And every minute you spend thinking about that is a minute you aren't looking for the real kidnapper!"

No kidding. Brittany glared at the agent. Didn't the man know how on edge they all were already? How could he even think this?

"Listen." Gary's voice bristled with indignation. He leaned forward and pointed at Agent Scarrow. "You hear me good. I had *nothing* to do with Shaley's kidnapping. I *don't know* how Fledger knew about the ring and the van."

Rayne flung out her arms. "This is insane—"

"Rayne, quiet! I don't need you to stand up for me."

"Of course I'm going to stand up for you!"

Gary sprang to his feet and faced Agent Scarrow. "I'm not answering any more of your questions, understand? I will not. Waste. Our. Time. If I have to, I'm calling a lawyer right now. You just find Shaley."

The agent sat back, one fist against his hip. He shot a rueful look at Gary, then Rayne. "All right. Sorry to upset you. Like I said, we have to check everything out." He stood and clicked off the recorder.

Anger and determination creased Rayne's face. "We want to announce the car and license plate at the press conference. And the kidnapper's name. You should find a picture of a 1997 blue Ford Explorer. Blow it up so the media can get a good shot of it. And blow up the mug shot of Fledger."

Agent Scarrow held up his palms. "Rayne, we're still discussing that."

"No!" She stuck out her chin. "Discussion's over. We've been sitting here for *twelve hours*, doing nothing but waiting for information from you. We can't wait any longer. We've made a decision; *we're* Shaley's parents, and we expect you to do what we want!"

You tell him, Rayne.

Gary lifted his hands, as if his outburst had drained him. "Rayne, it's okay. Calm down."

"I'm *not* going to calm down."

Agent Scarrow picked up his recorder and headed out of the room.

"How could he say that?" Brittany burst out, knowing full well the agent was still close enough to hear her.

"Come on, Rayne." Gary sat beside her and reached for her arm.

Rayne drew away. "Don't take his side, Gary. You heard what he was implying."

"It doesn't matter. He's just doing his job."

"It does matter."

"No, it doesn't." Gary reached for her again. "Come on, Rayne. It's okay."

Rayne's shoulders slumped. Her chin started to tremble. "Gary, I don't know what to do."

He nudged her toward him. Rayne gave in, sank against his chest, and burst into tears.

Brittany edged out of the room, heart breaking for them. She felt so helpless. If only she could make this all go away, right now.

As for Agent Scarrow — she wanted to punch the man.

My fingers shook so hard I could barely punch in the numbers. Nine.

My heart refused to beat. It quivered inside my ribs, flushing me with dizziness.

One. One.

I gripped the phone, smashing it against my ear. One ring.

"Nine-one-one, what is your emergency?"

I couldn't believe it. I was *talking* to someone!

"I — this is Shaley O'Connor." My voice came out in a whisper. "I've been kidnapped. Please help me. I'm somewhere in Utah, in a cabin."

"Are you okay?" The woman sounded so *calm*.

"Yes. No. *Please* come get me."

"We'll send someone, Shaley. Where were you kidnapped from?"

"Santa Barbara, California."

The woman hesitated. "You're Rayne's daughter?"

"Yes."

"Everyone's looking for you."

Really?

Of course it would be on the news by now. Still, just to hear people wanted to find me ...

"How many people are holding you, Shaley?"

"One man. He says his name is Joshua, but I doubt that's his real name. It's — "

"Is he still driving the Ford Explorer?"

I stifled a gasp. They knew that? We'd changed cars *twice*. "Yes."

"Okay. Can you stay on the phone?"

"I don't know the address. How do you know where to come?"

"We can see where you're calling from. We've already got people alerted."

Oh, thank you, God.

"Please tell my mom I didn't mean the things he made me say on the phone." My voice caught. Just the memory of saying those awful words ...

"I will."

I glanced over my shoulder toward the door.

"Where is Joshua right now, Shaley?"

"He's —"

On the other side of the wall, the toilet flushed. I jerked. "I have to go."

Footsteps in the bathroom. I heard the click of its door opening.

I set down the receiver — too fast. It rattled.

Heart in my throat, I flung myself left toward the closet. Yanked open the door and leaned down. I could hear Joshua coming.

His footsteps carved to a stop at the doorway. "*What* are you doing?"

I straightened up, gestured toward the closet. "It's empty. I was hoping to find shoes."

19

Brittany stood at the kitchen sink, filling a glass with water. Rayne stood beside her, stomach growling. Brittany knew Rayne had eaten nothing since two o'clock Saturday afternoon. Neither had Brittany. But how could they eat now? What if Shaley was going hungry? What kind of person would eat when her best friend couldn't?

Brittany gave the glass of water to Rayne and slipped an arm around her.

Rayne patted her shoulder. "Why don't you get some sleep?"

"You know I can't." Brittany looked toward the great room. "Where's Gary?"

"I don't know. In the den, I think."

Brittany rubbed her face and sighed. "I feel like ... dead. Or like my brain's been put in someone else's body. Everything isn't quite real."

Footsteps echoed on the great room floor. Hours ago the long rows of wedding chairs had been taken down, but only a few pieces of Ed's oversize furniture had been carted back in from the estate's storage shed. Now every sound in the huge room echoed.

"I know." Rayne took a long drink and set the glass in the sink. "Me too."

A cell phone went off from the dining room. Brittany froze. It was Agent Scarrow's — again. It rang all the time. And each time she feared hearing some terrible news. She cocked her head toward the sound.

"Scarrow."

Rayne caught Brittany's eye. They both remained still, listening.

"Oh," the agent said. "That's great news. Where?"

Rayne and Brittany exchanged wide-eyed looks and hurried out of the kitchen. At the threshold of the dining room they stopped, watching Agent Scarrow's face for clues. He sat near the end of the long table — his makeshift office — surrounded by files and papers and his laptop. As he talked he jotted in his notebook. He glanced at them and gave them a thumbs-up. Brittany's heart clutched. What? *What?*

She found Rayne's hand and gripped it.

Agent Scarrow scribbled on and on in his notepad. Brittany waited impatiently, drinking in his words. Something about a call. Local law enforcement sent out. He asked curt questions, then wrote some more.

Please God, please — have they found her?

"All right. Thanks. Get right back to me with updates." He ended the call and focused on Rayne, speaking rapidly. "Shaley called nine-one-one. She's in Utah."

"Oh!" Rayne's hand flew to her mouth.

Utah. For a split second Brittany's mind tripped over the detail. Shaley was now in *Utah*? Then crazy joy and relief flooded her body. She rushed forward, hands up, pleading. "Is she okay? Where is she?"

"In a cabin off Highway 125, southwest of Provo. Local law enforcement are on their way to seal off the cabin. Apparently Shaley managed to call while her kidnapper was somewhere else in the house. Sounded like she hung up abruptly when she heard him coming."

"Can they get to her?" Rayne's voice sounded tinny.

"The sheriff's department is cordoning off the property. The FBI's field office in Salt Lake City is two hours' drive north. They've got a SWAT unit. We're calling in the unit to handle the situation. These are very highly trained men. They'll get the job done."

SWAT unit?

Questions crammed into Brittany's mind. So many things could go wrong.

"But those men are *two hours* away?" Rayne dug her fingers into her hair. "And that's once they're called in and ready to go. Why not have the local police —"

"They're out in the sticks, near a small town of seven hundred people. Local police don't have the resources to do what we need. The FBI's SWAT team will know how to negotiate, how to talk a suspect into giving up. And if they have to, they know how to storm the place and remove Shaley."

Where was Gary? He should be hearing this. Brittany swiveled toward the great room. "I'll go tell everyone!"

She ran through the great room, shouting, "They know where Shaley is, they *know* where she is!" Bedroom doors opened on the second floor. Gary darted out of the den. "What happened?" He ran toward Brittany.

"She called nine-one-one!"

Band members and Ed Schering spilled from their rooms, their footsteps pounding down the two big staircases. Brittany led them all into the dining room. Soon they were grouped around Agent Scarrow and Rayne, questions tumbling from them. He went over the story once again. Rayne held on to Gary, whispering, "God heard our prayers."

Yes, he did, Brittany thought. But what would that evil man who'd kidnapped Shaley do when he found himself surrounded by a SWAT team?

Rayne let go of Gary and grabbed Al's wrist. "How long until they get there?"

"As you mentioned, the team needs to assemble and be briefed on the situation before heading out. It's a two-hour drive, but they'll transport to the site in a chopper. So altogether they should be at the cabin within two hours."

Two hours. That would be six o'clock Pacific time. Tears filled Brittany's eyes. It was good news. But two hours was an *eternity*.

"They'll get her, Rayne." Gary's voice shook. "They'll bring Shaley home."

20

A ringing phone jangled thirty-two-year-old Randy Sullivan from a sound sleep. His arm shot out to snatch up the receiver almost before the first ring stopped. It was an automatic reflex, honed from many nights of being jangled awake.

He pressed the phone to his ear, propped up on one elbow. "Sullivan."

"We need you here pronto. Mission near Oak City, southwest of Provo." Bear's voice — the SWAT unit leader.

The line went dead.

Sullivan heaved out of bed, fully awake.

The bed covers rustled. "You have to go?" His wife's voice, thick from sleep, filtered through the darkness.

"Yeah."

A small intake of breath from Rhonda. No matter how many missions he went on, she always worried. With good reason. "Be careful," she said.

"Always."

Randy strode to the bathroom by the light of the corner streetlamp filtering through the bedroom window. He dressed in one minute flat. His uniform and gear were already in the car, ready at a minute's notice — the military-issued bulletproof vest, the helmet and goggles, the weapons and accessories. Exactly what he took would depend on the mission. At the Stable — his team's slang for their headquarters — Bear would brief them on the situation.

Before leaving the bedroom, he bent down to kiss his wife's cheek. She felt warm and smooth. "Love you."

She reached up, placed a palm against his cheek. "Come back to me."

"Always."

Two years ago, one of his team members *hadn't* come back.

Randy hurried down the hall past the room where their two-year-old, Stevie, slept. As he passed the open door, he brushed fingertips against the doorjamb. "Hug you, Stevie," he whispered.

A moment later, the garage door opened, and Randy started his Bronco and backed out. The neighborhood streets were quiet and empty. Randy drank in the peace. He wouldn't have it for long.

Within ten minutes he'd reached the Stable. Soon all of the men on his team had showed up.

"Hey, Crooner." Randy's nickname was an inside joke, as were all the other men's. Bear, their team leader, had heard him singing off-key as he worked out one day, and Crooner he became.

"Okay, we're all here. Heads up, we gotta move." Bear stood in front of them and next to a flip chart, notes in hand for the mission briefing. The top sheet on the chart showed a hand-drawn view of roads and a small house.

Bear stood six foot four, with the shoulders and chest of a bear — hence his nickname. His thick brown hair finished the image. "You all hear on the news yesterday about Shaley O'Connor's kidnap just before her parents' wedding?"

Heard it? Randy's eyebrows went up. *Every* channel was full of the story.

"We get to go rescue her."

"You're kiddin' me." Eagle's beady eyes lit. Murmurs went around the room.

"Man, I *love* Rayne's music," Volt said. Volt — short for voltage — was tall and lean and ran like the wind. A long lightning bolt tattoo jagged down his left arm.

Randy exchanged a meaningful look with Coop, whose nickname came from his long chicken neck. They both knew what a case like this meant: publicity, and lots of it. They'd better dot every *i* and cross every *t*. Not that they usually didn't. But with the national media breathing down your back ...

Bear ignored the comments. "She's in a rural cabin off Highway 125. Held by one HT — calling himself Joshua." HT — short for hostage taker. "We've been informed his real name is Ronald Fledger. Spent a year and a half in prison for stalking Shaley.

"Fledger is fifty-five years old. You may have seen the suspect's composite on TV. Here's a look at the real guy, before he got the hair cut off in prison." Bear handed a copy of Fledger's mug shot to Rex, who gave it a good look and passed it to Randy.

He studied the picture. Ugly man. Mean-looking small eyes and disgustingly big lips. Randy shook his head. He couldn't imagine his own child stolen by a man like this.

"And here's one of Miss O'Connor." Bear gave a second sheet to Rex.

Randy leaned toward Rex and studied the photo. Same one he'd seen on the news. A close-up. He'd spotted the picture on some grocery store tabloid in the past. Randy gazed at the photo not because he didn't know what Shaley looked like — he'd seen her face dozens of times — but because he wanted to memorize every detail. To hold those eyes in his memory. This girl's safety was why he'd been pulled out of bed. Right now she depended on his team and their years of vigorous training — for her life.

"We've got the sheriff's department on the scene." Bear handed a small stack of papers to Rex. "Each of you, take one. They faxed this map and layout of the cabin and surrounding roads. It's up here too." He tapped the flip chart. "Small wooden cabin, porch with two steps. Two levels. Only one door entry — the one on the porch." He pointed to the spot. "Detached, windowless garage to the left of the cabin."

Randy's trained eyes took in the sheet he held in his hands, then the bigger flip-chart view. He noted every window in the cabin, the measured distance between the house and woods and garage, the proposed location of the command post. Forest was a good thing. Trees meant cover.

For the next five minutes, Bear continued talking. Randy knew the importance of the briefing. All the same he could feel the moments slipping by — and every one had to seem an eternity to Shaley O'Connor.

Hold on, Shaley. We're coming.

Briefing over, the men hurried to change into their uniforms and pull equipment from their cars. The uniform and boots were camouflage, with a large FBI insignia on the upper arms. Over that went the bulletproof vest, which held numerous pieces of equipment and magazine pouches for extra ammunition.

Randy checked his submachine gun, his main weapon. A waist belt with thigh harness held an extra, smaller gun.

The mission also called for a gas mask, plus eye and ear protection in case they had to throw a flash-bang into the cabin. Those things were so bright and loud that any unprotected person, including Shaley, would be stunned right down to the floor. She'd be blinded for about five seconds. Not the way they wanted to treat any innocent victim, but sometimes they had to do it to catch the bad guy.

Randy would put on his helmet and affix the radio to his ear after reaching the site.

Team assembled and ready, they climbed into a transport vehicle to take them to the waiting chopper.

On the short drive, Randy went over in his mind what was to come. Eight highly trained, excellent marksmen against one out-of-shape fifty-five-year-old man. Sounded like a slam-dunk. But no mission was routine, especially with a hostage involved. You just couldn't predict what a man might do when he was up against a wall. When his only choices were surrender and jail — or death.

Sometimes they chose death.

And sometimes they took their hostages with them.

21

Don't lie to me, Shaley," Joshua spat. "You weren't looking for shoes."

His eyes narrowed as I cringed by the bedroom closet. For a terrifying moment we faced off. My heart was about to bang out of my chest.

"Yes, I was."

He strode toward me. "You picked up the phone, didn't you?" He caught my arm and squeezed.

"No!"

"I heard the *phone*!"

"You didn't!" My head jerked toward the closet. "You heard this door open."

Joshua's stale breath poured over me, his anger buzzing like bees. "Who'd you talk to?"

"Nobody!"

"*Who?*" He yanked me close to him, his face inches from mine. In his eyes I saw hatred and betrayal deep enough to kill. My stomach shriveled.

"I didn't talk to *anyone*!"

He cursed and shoved me away from him. I hit the wall. "You've really done it now, Shaley. If anybody comes here to rescue you — you're dead."

22

Randy and his team reached the target area at 6:55 a.m. They'd landed in an open field a good distance from the cabin — so as not to alert the HT — then were driven in by sheriff's department vehicles.

Sheriff's deputies had blocked off the narrow dirt road to the cabin. The road rounded a bend about a quarter mile away, disappearing into forest.

They piled out of the vehicles and were quickly introduced to three men who'd had a chance to survey the area firsthand. Bart Stockle from the Utah State Police shook Bear's hand. Stockle was commander of the mission and would make the decisions regarding the SWAT unit's actions. "Glad you guys are here. I arrived just a short time ago. Still gathering information."

Off to Randy's left sat the mobile command post brought down from the state police in Provo. The large vehicle contained all the communications equipment needed to link every member of the three agencies involved in the mission. Radio would be used, since the guys manning the command post couldn't be close enough to see the action. Randy and his unit, plus all the men from the two other agencies, were their eyes and ears. Randy's radio transmitter, housed in a pouch on his shoulder, attached to an earpiece via a clear cord.

"All right." Rich Adams, from the sheriff's department, pointed up the dirt road. "Cabin's about a third of a mile up, around that bend." He held up a large, hand-drawn map, similar to the small ones Bear had handed out. "We've got men here, here, and here." He pointed to areas around the cabin. "First responder arrived within five minutes of the call. He and backups stopped here and went in on foot. There's no other way out of the cabin but this road. And it's been manned since then. We've got snipers in the woods on all sides of the cabin.

"No vehicle outside the cabin. The HT's stolen Ford Explorer apparently is in the closed detached garage. There are no windows to the garage. In the darkness one of our men crept close enough to the cabin to hear voices, so we know they're in there. All windows in the cabin are closed. Front door entrance only."

Adams set down the map and picked up a set of blueprints. Randy knew the local guys had been busy while he and the team were in the chopper. Some unlucky clerk at the building department had no doubt been awakened by the sheriff's department with an immediate request — blueprints for the cabin.

Stockle moved to hold up one side of the large blueprints.

"Okay." Adams pointed to the document. "First level is essentially one big room. Den here, kitchen here." His finger slid left. "Over here on the right — stairs. Upstairs, we have ..." Stockle let go of his side, and Adams flipped to the second page. "Long hall and two bedrooms with a bathroom in the middle. Two windows in the hall. Bedroom windows here." He pointed to numerous locations. "One window in the bathroom."

Adams turned to Bear. "What's your assessment?"

Bear eyed the map. "We can't know what floor they're on. Now that it's light it's not feasible to get a man across the clearing and able to check through a window without the possibility of being seen. Surprise isn't the way to go." Bear looked at Chuck Trayna, the man serving as negotiator.

"All right." Stockle nodded. "I say it's time we make ourselves known and talk him out of there." He looked to Adams. "The cabin phone — who's it registered under?"

"John Baynor. Whereabouts unknown. Apparently he's not at the cabin."

Stockle repeated the name to himself. "What do we know about Baynor?"

"Short rap sheet: petty theft, that kind of thing. Worked as a clerk in a small hardware store in town until a week ago. He gave notice, said it was effective immediately, and hasn't been seen since. Oh, and he gave away his dog to a friend."

Gave away his dog? Guy must have had some kind of plans.

Stockle considered the information. "But he's not our guy."

"Nope," Adams replied. "It's Fledger for sure. Maybe he knows Fledger. Or maybe Fledger just happened to stumble upon his empty cabin."

Randy gazed down the dirt road. His uniform was hot and heavy. Fully loaded with weapons, he would be carrying forty-five pounds. *Hang in there, Shaley. You'll be rescued soon.*

Stockle nodded decisively. "All right. Let's get this team in place and make a phone call."

23

Randy was sweating by the time the cabin appeared around the bend. He and his unit moved in a loping run, silent and with heads down, guns in their hands.

Bear signaled for them to stop. Every man skidded to a halt, eyes on their leader. He pointed to various members of the unit, then indicated what direction they should go. Randy peeled off to the right with Coop, Rex, and Volt. The plan was to diffuse into the forest, using tree cover to approach the cabin. They'd have two men on all four sides. Once surrounding the target, they'd position to fire. The procedure did not call for complete stealth. On the contrary, they wanted the HT to know they were there. Their presence and firepower sent a very clear message — *you are outnumbered.*

Randy skulked through the trees, followed by the other three. His heart beat double, and his hands gripped the gun. No matter how hard the training, how much experience he'd had, every mission sent his blood pumping.

At the clearing Randy and Coop veered toward the side of the cabin. Rex and Volt ran on toward the back.

Randy positioned himself behind the first tree at the edge of the clearing. The cabin sat a mere thirty feet away. He keyed his radio and spoke quietly. "Crooner and Coop ready."

Some ten feet away, behind another tree, a sniper crouched. The insignia on his uniform read *Utah State Police.* If negotiations went south and they had to go tactical — storm the cabin — the snipers would provide cover as the SWAT unit moved in to breach the door.

In the next minute voices on the TAC channel sounded in Randy's ear.

"Volt and Rex ready."

Shaley, just a little while longer. He pictured the teen freed, calling her mom. Randy couldn't wait to see that.

"Bray and Starsky ready." Cover for those two would be the garage, on the other side of the cabin.

"Bear and Eagle ready."

Eight law enforcement vehicles, both from the sheriff's department and Utah State Police, gunned up the dirt road. Two of them carried the rest of the SWAT unit's gear in their backseats — masks, ear protection, and other equipment needed if the team had to go tactical. For now the men did not wear the masks, as they decreased visibility. The cars slid to a halt, kicking up dust, lined up one behind the other. A man leapt out of each car and squatted behind it, weapon aimed at the target. One of them was Adams.

Shaley's kidnapper had to be feeling the heat about now. What would he do?

From inside the cabin, Randy heard the phone start to ring.

One jangle. Two ... three ... four ... Randy lost count after ten.

He knew Trayna was phoning from the command post, Stockle by his side. If the HT didn't answer the phone, Trayna would move behind the sheriff's department vehicles and use the megaphone. But that would be a one-sided conversation. Always better to engage the HT, try to win his trust. It was the best chance of persuading him to give up.

The phone rang and rang ... then stopped. Randy exchanged a glance with Coop. Not good, but not unexpected. It could take hours for an HT to decide to talk. Hours more to convince him to surrender.

The phone started ringing again.

Randy thought of Rhonda and Stevie. They'd be getting up about now. Stevie would be eating breakfast — pancakes, since it was Sunday. Rhonda would make him a special one in a heart shape. Stevie loved that. He'd insist on buttering it himself. And he'd pour on too much syrup.

Ten rings … twelve … more.

Randy squinted at the cabin windows. He saw no peering face, no hand with a gun. What was happening inside? Randy shifted on his feet. This was the hard part — waiting.

Time ticked by. The phone rang and stopped, rang and stopped. After half an hour, Randy heard Stockle's voice in his ear. "We've giving up on calling. Moving in to megaphone."

Soon a sheriff's deputy car drove up behind the others and stopped. Trayna got out. Using the cover of all the cars, he stooped low and made his way as close to the cabin as possible.

"Ronald Fledger!" Trayna's amplified voice split the quiet morning air. "This is Chuck Trayna from the Utah State Police. We want you to come out with your hands behind your head. We have the cabin surrounded. The best way out of this for you is to come out quietly. Nobody will be hurt."

The words faded away — then silence.

Randy focused on the windows, seeing nothing.

Stockle waited a few minutes, then tried again.

No response.

A third time. No response. Just agonizing quiet.

Sweat trickled down Randy's neck. The longer the silence, the more likely they would hear the sound they all prayed wouldn't come — one shot in the cabin, followed by a second.

The HT's murder of his victim, then his suicide.

Randy held Shaley's image in his mind. So young. So much to live for. A cold feeling crept through his gut. Something was wrong inside. Very wrong. They should have seen something, heard *something* by now. Even if the HT shouted at them to go away. Better to hear him curse and rave than this impenetrable *silence*.

Trayna tried again and again. Each time — nothing.

Randy and Coop exchanged another glance. The time was coming for Plan C. They could feel it.

Trayna lowered his megaphone and fully disappeared behind the deputy's car.

No words in Randy's earpiece. Most likely Trayna was on the second channel that connected him to Stockle and Bear. As commander of the mission, it was Stockle's decision alone to make the call to go tactical.

In the lull birds sang in the forest, and a breeze ruffled the weeds around the cabin.

What was happening in there? What was the HT planning?

Randy let his eyes glide over the deputies behind their cars, pistols aimed at the cabin. He could see Rex and Volt in their positions at the rear. He couldn't see the other four on the team, but he knew they were there, weapons ready. All those guns. All that ammunition. And one seventeen-year-old victim who could so easily get caught in the crossfire.

A crackle in Randy's ear. Bear's voice came over the channel. "Stockle just gave me the green light. We're moving in."

f anybody comes here to rescue you — you're dead."

I gaped at Joshua, his words echoing in my head. The 9-1-1 operator had said the police were on their way. Now it was too late to stop them.

Joshua caught my wrist in a viselike grip and swung toward the bedroom door. With a jerk he pulled me behind him. "Come on," he growled.

I stumbled after him, sick and trembling. Up the hall he dragged me, then down the stairs. Tears blurred my eyes. We hit the first landing. I tripped and fell into Joshua. He grabbed a bunch of my hair and pulled me up like a broken doll. I yelped. He shoved me over to the couch and pushed me down. "Sit. Don't move."

I cringed on the dingy sofa, head hanging.

Joshua stomped over to the TV and smacked it on. Punched the channel button again and again. Was he searching for news? Fear chewed at me. Surely my call wouldn't be on the news this fast ...

All we saw were commercials.

Joshua ran into the kitchen. Rummaged through drawers. With a grunt he banged the last one shut and strode back to me, carrying a three-foot piece of rope. "Gimme your hands."

I did as I was told. He wound the rope around my wrists, a sneer on his face. "Thought you could beat me, didn't you. Thought you could get away. Guess what, Shaley. *No* one's taking you away from me alive. Not *ever.*"

B rittany slumped in a chair next to Rayne in the great room, numbly watching through the rear windows as sunlight leaked into the backyard.

At five in the morning Ed Schering, needing something to do, had rounded up Rayne's three bodyguards plus his own security guys to bring down the great room furniture from the storage shed. Now all the Rayne band members, including the three backup singers, were gathered with Agent Scarrow in the big room. Some stood, some paced. Carly, Shaley's favorite backup singer, sat with her dark head bowed — probably praying. Kim and Morrey huddled together on a couch. Ross stood with legs apart and arms folded, gazing out the back windows at the rear gardens.

Agent Scarrow stood near the wall, one hand rubbing his lips. His phone — their connection to news, the bright possibility of this horrible nightmare ending — sat clipped to his belt.

Tension vibrated the room. No one spoke.

Feeling wooden and heavy, Brittany turned her gaze to the floor. A dozen terrible scenarios whirled in her head. Shaley, killed by her kidnapper. Or caught in the crossfire of her rescuers. Shot dead . . . wounded . . . paralyzed for life.

God, please get her out of there safely!

Agent Scarrow's phone rang. Brittany jumped.

Every person in the great room tensed. Every pair of eyes snapped to the FBI agent.

He pulled the phone from his belt. "Scarrow."

Brittany clutched Rayne's hand. Her heart whirred into erratic beats.

"Okay." Agent Scarrow focused across the room. He wouldn't look at Rayne. Did that mean something? *Why* wouldn't he *look* at her?

"Yeah." He nodded. "Okay. Thanks."

He punched the *end* button and lowered the phone. Finally he met Rayne's gaze.

Stop! Brittany thought. *Stop, don't tell us!* What she heard next could kill her — and *she didn't want to know . . .*

Gary wrapped an arm around Rayne's shoulder. His breathing sounded ragged.

Agent Scarrow spread his hands. "They can't get an answer out of the suspect. The SWAT unit is moving in."

"Unnhh!" Rayne let out a wail. Gary clung to her, still as a stone. Kim gasped, and Ross uttered a curse. Brittany couldn't move. Couldn't talk or cry. Rayne's head slowly turned toward her, and they locked eyes.

Within minutes, this horrible nightmare would finally be over.

But would Shaley still be alive?

26

At Bear's command, Randy and Coop abandoned their positions in the forest, as did the other men in the unit. Within one minute they had regrouped, taking cover behind the deputies' cars. Double the adrenaline now pumped through Randy's veins. Storming the cabin was necessary but so risky. So many things could go wrong.

Bear spoke low and rapidly, telling them the plan. "Okay." He nodded. "Mask up."

From the backseats of the two vehicles, they pulled their extra gear. Volt carried an attachment for his weapon — the XM – 26, which used short-range, nonlethal bullets that could turn a door's lock into dust. Once the breach was complete, Volt would transition his weapon to fire lethal bullets.

Randy pulled on his mask and fixed the protection over his ears. Outside sounds muted. He could hear the thump of his heart. Sheriff's deputies on scene donned their own ear protection.

Crouching down, the men formed their lineup. Bear signaled *go* to the two state policemen, who'd put on their own similar gear. They took off toward the woods to circle behind the house.

Randy gripped his MP5, every muscle in his body gathered to spring.

Seconds ticked by. Randy envisioned the two officers. They'd be reaching the rear woods by now, taking out their flash-bangs. When they threw the grenades to create a distraction, they'd look away, eyes closed —

Bang, bang! Through his ear protection, Randy heard the muted explosions.

"Go!" Bear's command.

Randy jumped up and stacked against the man in front of him. In a tight unit, they ran toward the front door. They flew up two steps. Volt veered to the left side of the door, Rex toward the right. Volt raised his weapon and fired at the lock at a forty-five degree angle. The lock disintegrated. He kicked in the door.

Rex threw in a flash-bang.

Randy jerked his head away, closed his eyes.

The stun grenade exploded.

Bray stormed inside, gun raised. The rest of the team pressed in after him.

Every man peeled off in his specified direction.

Randy jumped inside the cabin behind Coop, his eyes glued to his target — the staircase to the right. In the split second it took him to reach the bottom step, he sensed the quick movements of Bray and Starsky as they cleared the downstairs.

No gunfire.

Randy pounded up the steps.

In front of him, Coop swerved left. Randy stayed inches behind him.

Bear and Eagle cleared the threshold of the first door and ran inside. Coop and Randy sprinted to the second. Weapon up, Coop checked around the doorjamb, then burst inside. Randy followed.

Small bathroom.

Tub, sink, toilet.

Clear.

They returned to the hall.

Still no gunshots. Vaguely, Randy heard the men in the second bedroom.

"Downstairs clear." Bray's voice in Randy's ear.

"First bedroom clear."

Randy keyed his radio. "Bathroom clear."

He looked toward the second bedroom. The only place left.

Rex stepped into the hall. "Second bedroom clear."

Randy's muscles sagged. No way. The cabin was *empty*?

No HT, no Shaley.

Mission over.

Just like that.

Everything in Randy's body slowed as his adrenaline tried to dissipate. He shook his head at Coop. He still couldn't believe it.

"There's a TV on down here." Bray again. He cussed, sounding like Randy felt — crushed. "Must be the voices the deputy heard."

Randy leaned against the wall and let out a long breath. They'd failed. The HT had escaped — hours ago. And Shaley O'Connor would now be in more danger than ever.

27

I lay on my side in the third-row seats of the Explorer, hands still bound with rough rope. The fibers bit into my wrists, and my head pounded. My whole body felt weak. Dully, I gazed at the back of the dirty beige seat in front of me, the scene at the cabin playing over and over in my mind.

I never should have called 9-1-1.

After Joshua had tied my hands, he slammed out the cabin's front door, pulling me with him. "We're leavin' now. No rest for us here — thanks to you."

We didn't even stop to turn off the TV.

He hauled me to the garage, pulled up the door and jerked me inside. Getting into the Explorer was harder with bound hands. Joshua pushed me in and ordered me to the third row. "Lie down on the floor."

He backed out the SUV, then hopped out to close the garage door. We sped away from the cabin so fast I was sure we'd crash.

That was, what, two hours ago? It was just turning light outside. I couldn't tell if the sun had risen.

How long would this go on? What would happen when we stopped next?

At least the police knew what kind of car we were driving. They'd be looking for it. Did they know the license plate? Why hadn't anyone found us by now?

My stomach felt so empty. And I needed water.

I couldn't live like this.

My eyes closed, tears squeezing through my lids. Fact was — maybe I wouldn't.

It wasn't something I'd allowed myself to think about before. But the more I tried to push it away, the stronger the feeling grew. The police knew our car and they knew the cabin. Still, Joshua had gotten away. And he was going to kill me. Maybe today. Maybe tomorrow or next week. But I could never become the subservient wife living in the wilderness that he wanted me to become. If he thought he'd brainwash me to believe in his false Christianity, he was in for a surprise. I wouldn't. *Ever.*

One day he was going to get tired of my fighting.

"Shaley!" Joshua barked.

I tensed. "What."

"I'm going to stop soon. We'll get a different car. I don't want you to *move* until I tell you to, hear? Then you're going to do exactly what I say."

"I have to go to the bathroom."

No answer.

"Joshua!"

"Shut up."

Get a different car. The words registered. How was he going to do that?

From deep inside me, a new voice whispered. The voice of justice.

Minutes ticked by. The voice grew stronger.

If I didn't live through this, never saw Mom and Dad again, there was one thing I could do — make sure this man paid for what he did to me. Make sure he wasn't free to kidnap someone else.

I needed to leave evidence. A trail of clues to prove where I'd been, what Joshua had done.

Vengeance and anger washed over me. It felt good, energizing. I *could* do something, even kidnapped and with my hands tied.

The Explorer slowed.

Reaching up with my bound hands, I stuck out my right thumb and pressed it hard against the bottom of the window.

I brought my hands to my hair, still loosely bound in the rubber band. Took hold of a small lock and pulled. Pain scratched my skull. I didn't care. I pulled harder. The hairs came out. I dropped them on the floor.

Our car turned right, then bumped over an entrance.

I swallowed. "Where are we?"

"I told you to shut up."

The Explorer stopped. I held my breath. Joshua's seat squeaked as he got out. His door slammed.

Silence.

Heart thudding, I dared to half sit up and peek through my window.

We were in a parking lot behind some big store. Joshua stood with his back to me by a maroon four-door car that faced the opposite direction of the Explorer. He was doing something to the driver's door.

Breaking into the car.

The door opened. Joshua pulled up straight and glanced around. I ducked back down in my seat.

A short time later I heard a motor start.

How did he *do* that?

The engine kept running. Joshua's footsteps came around the rear of the Explorer. The back door opened.

"Get out," he snapped. "Hurry."

I sat up and wriggled my way to the end of the seat. Pushed to my feet and struggled forward. Joshua caught my tied wrists and pulled me down to the pavement. "Move." He shoved me around the Explorer and to the maroon car. Opened the back door. "Get down on the seat."

I slid inside and lay down. Joshua slammed the door.

More noises came from the SUV. Joshua opening up the back? A door on the Explorer closed. Joshua reached into the driver's seat of our new car, seeking a button. The trunk popped open.

I heard a muffled thump as he threw things inside.

A suitcase? His possessions? I'd never even looked in the back of that SUV.

The trunk closed. Joshua ran around and jumped into the car. With a surge of the engine, we took off.

Only then did the realization fully hit me. The police would be looking for the Explorer. They wouldn't know about this car — my new prison. And Joshua would be free to take me farther and farther away.

As the sun rose, streaming light from the passenger side windows, I lay on the seat and cried. There was no help for me now.

Mom, Dad. I'll never see you again.

I had no strength even to pray. But the voice of vengeance inside me did. The voice begged God that he'd lead the police to the Explorer. That they'd discover my hair and the fingerprint. And that they would know Shaley O'Connor had once been there.

ayne sat on a couch in the great room, holding hands with
Gary on her right and Brittany on her left. Ross, Carly and the
two other backup singers, Ed Schering, and the band members had
shoved furniture together to form a circle.

For an eternity they waited for Al's phone to ring. When it finally
did, Rayne dropped Brittany's and Gary's hands and pressed both
fists to her chest.

Al turned away and answered the call.

In the seconds that followed, Rayne imagined herself rising from
her chair and floating away. This body she was in — the jagging
nerves and runaway heart — it wasn't hers. For the millionth time
since Shaley's kidnapping, Rayne told herself none of this was real.
It just. Couldn't. Be.

"Okay," Al said. Was that disappointment in his voice? Rayne
peered at him, waiting for some sign. A thumbs-up. A smile.

Nothing.

"Let me inform the family, then I'll get back to you." Al snapped
off his phone and faced Rayne.

Her pulse stopped.

"When they entered the cabin, Fledger and Shaley were gone."

A bright sword pierced Rayne's head. Her lungs deflated as if all
air had been sucked from the room. No. Not after all this waiting.
All this time. *Wasted.*

Gray amorphous dots crowded into her vision. Rayne's stomach turned over. Her body slowly pitched forward toward the floor.

Strong arms caught her. Rayne's head lulled to the side.

The world faded to black.

Long after Joshua had peeled out of the parking lot in our maroon sedan, I finally cried myself out. My wrists burned from the rope, and my head swam from lying down so long. My despair subsided, leaving me once again to think about how I could save myself.

As for Joshua — he had to be tired. He'd been up all night. The man had to sleep sometime. But when he did, no doubt he'd tie me up so tight I wouldn't be able to move at all.

I had to get on his good side.

It was my only choice. Somehow I had to pretend I was bonding with him. Had to make him think I'd never try to escape again. Then I'd wait for his guard to drop.

Meanwhile I'd leave as many clues behind as possible.

Little by little I gathered courage until — on spur of the moment — I sat up in the backseat. I was taking a huge risk in disobeying. But I just couldn't lie there forever.

"Hey," Joshua growled at me. "Get back down."

"I can't. Really. I *have* to go to the bathroom."

Surely he had to go too. From the middle of the backseat, I peered at what I could see of his profile. He was sweating, and his fat jowls seemed to droop more than ever. If he drove much longer, he just might crash and kill us both.

"I'll stop soon enough." Even Joshua's voice dragged. "Gonna have to get gas."

My gaze snagged on something on the floor by Joshua's feet. I leaned forward and tilted my head.

His gun.

Would he shoot me in the back if I tried to run?

Through the front windshield, I saw a divided highway — a much bigger road than many we'd taken. Farmland to our right and left. A sign said *Highway 20*. Was that in Utah?

"Where's the closest gas station?"

"There's a town a few miles up. We'll stop there."

I met his eyes through the rearview mirror. They were bloodshot. "You need to sleep."

"Yeah, tell me about it. Thanks to *you*."

My chin dipped, and I looked at my lap. "I'm sorry."

Joshua snorted.

"I *am*. Do you think I'm happy to have this rope cutting into my wrists? It really hurts. And I don't want you mad at me."

"You should have thought about that before you picked up the phone."

"I know."

Silence. My bladder was so full my back throbbed. Each mile was an eternity.

"Joshua." I hated the sound of his name on my tongue. "What do you want me to do when we stop?"

"Won't know till we get there."

I gazed at him, an amazing thought leaking into my head. After his intensive planning to steal me in a jeweler's van right off a guarded estate, now he didn't seem to know what happened next. He obviously hadn't expected something to go wrong. And he had no Plan B.

Every good schemer had a Plan B.

I could use this. How, I didn't know yet. But I would use it.

The clock on the dashboard read 9:35 a.m. That would be Utah time. If we had still been in the Explorer, the clock would have read 8:35. The Explorer's was the time that counted. It was California time. *Home* time.

"What state are we in?" I asked.

"Idaho."

Idaho. A long state. Were we still in south Idaho?

I told myself we were. Southern Idaho was closer to Mom and Dad than northern Idaho.

Finally ahead I saw a sign for the town of Rigby. "Please stop. Just tell me what you want me to do, and I'll do it."

"Say nothin' to nobody, that's what. Walk with your head down like before."

"You'll need to cut off these ropes."

We reached the town. Joshua slowed and turned off the highway, following a sign for a gas station. We drove down a street with businesses on either side. People were on the sidewalks, going in and out of buildings. So close to me. As we stopped at a red light, one woman even met my eyes. Silently, I pleaded with her. *Have you seen my picture on the news? It's me, Shaley! Help me!*

For a hovering second, I thought I'd fling myself toward the door, tumble out of the car. But my hands were tied, and the door no doubt was locked. And that gun by his feet . . .

The woman turned away. My heart sank.

With a dull stare I focused out the windshield. "There's the gas station."

"I see it."

Joshua pulled into the station and parked on the far side, away from other cars. He opened the glove compartment and took out a folded knife. Flicked it open. The blade shot out, six inches long and glistening.

I stilled. The whole time we'd been in the Explorer, I hadn't known he had that.

Joshua hoisted around in his seat. "Put your hands on the console."

After a long look into his eyes, I obeyed.

He brought the knife to the rope, and in two quick slices cut through it. The relief from that tightness! Joshua unwound the pieces and tossed them on the floor. I pressed fingers around one throbbing wrist, then gasped at the even greater pain. The raw skin felt like a burn.

Joshua focused over my shoulder through the back windshield. "Bathrooms are on this side. I'll take you now. Then we're walking back to the car, and I'll get gas." He gave me a hard look.

"Okay."

We got out of the car and walked straight to the bathrooms, Joshua's arm brushing against mine. He smelled of grime and sweat. Joshua knocked on the door to the ladies' room, heard no reply, then opened it. Looked inside. A one-toilet bathroom. "Go." He pushed my back. "Don't lock it."

I scurried inside, ready to pop, thanking God I'd made it. Even after I was done using the toilet, my lower back still hurt. I washed my hands, avoiding the mirror. I glanced around, wishing there was some way I could leave a message. But I had nothing to write with, nothing to use to scratch the wall. And if I took too long, Joshua would come in to check.

Reluctantly I stepped back outside. Joshua stood waiting. "Don't you have to go?"

He gave me a twisted smile. "Already did, while you were in there. You think I'd leave you alone?"

Grasping my elbow, he propelled me back to the sedan. "Head down."

My chin dropped, but my eyes looked up toward the license plate. From the state of Utah. As we drew closer I could read *Olympic Winter Games 2002* below the plate numbers. To the left was the five-ring circle logo of the Olympics. I stared at the numbers and letters, branding them into my brain. Only five to remember, so much easier than a California plate.

478B2 ... 478B2 ... 478B2 ...

Once again in the backseat, I repeated the sequence again and again in my head. *478B2 ...*

This one I wouldn't forget.

Joshua reconnected some wires to start the engine, turned

around, and pulled to a pump. There were only two, and the other sat empty. Vaguely, I wondered what I would do if another customer drove up. Hands now untied, I could be out of the car and screaming so fast—

Joshua picked the gun off the floor, leaned back in his seat, and shoved it under the waistband of his pants. Through the rearview mirror he aimed a tight-lipped, meaningful glare at me.

"I know."

As he filled the car with gas, I didn't dare move.

When he finished he opened the back door on the passenger side, leaned down. "Get in the front seat."

Why? almost slipped from my lips. I bit it back and did as I was told.

We drove out of Rigby and back into wilderness. I felt like I left half my heart in that little town. So close to people and rescue, yet so very far.

I stared at the road uncoiling before us and tried not to cry.

I n the backseat of Ed Schering's personal limo, Rayne clutched Gary's hand. Police cars escorted them, front and back. "It's going to be a zoo out there," Al had warned them. "The media are all over this story."

Rayne was used to the melee of reporters. Usually she disliked it. Today she was grateful. Anything to get the word out about Shaley. Someone out there would spot her. They *would*.

Rayne, Gary, and Al were the only ones in the limo. Brittany, Ross, and the band members wanted to go, to stand behind Rayne and Gary as a line of support. But that would have been too many people and would have required all the more police to guard them all. Even the three bodyguards had been left behind.

The press conference was set for ten o'clock in the morning at the Santa Barbara County courthouse on Anacapa Street. It would be live on TV, with every national network and cable news channel carrying it. Many local stations as well.

Rayne's watch now read 9:45. They'd been informed the micro-phones were all in place. One of Al's colleagues from the field office was bringing a blown-up picture of Shaley and a large mug shot of Ronald Fledger. Gary and Rayne would be escorted to the mics, say their piece, and leave. Al would stay behind to field questions. He would include information about the color and make of the car, and the suspect. Every eye out there would be looking for an old blue Ford Explorer and a man behind its wheel matching Fledger's description.

God, may someone find the car soon.

In the hours following the failed SWAT mission, Rayne's endurance had crumbled. But she forced her mind from terrifying imaginings to a constructive task—writing her press conference speech. Gary and Al had helped.

That speech now lay folded in the small purse slung over her shoulder. The FBI didn't want her and Gary to appear threatening or vengeful. If the kidnapper saw that, he might react in anger—and Shaley would pay. They were to speak quietly, in control, and to Shaley's kidnapper. They were to plead for their daughter's safe return.

The pleading part would not be hard.

Rayne's eyes burned, and her nerves felt like sandpaper, her lungs weighted with exhaustion. Every breath was an effort. Each minute she thought, *I can't live through the next one.* Then, somehow, she did.

"There's the front of the courthouse." Al pointed.

A distant *whop-whop* sounded in the air. Rayne didn't need to see the helicopter to register the sound. Some TV station, no doubt.

In the next block, she saw a long series of white stucco buildings with red roofs on her left, looking much like an old Spanish mission. A tower with a large clock rose from the front entrance. Palm trees around the buildings blew in a slight breeze.

Such a pretty sight. On such a horrible day.

The limo stopped at the intersection. The side street where they needed to turn left had been blocked off by police. The police car ahead of them turned, and the barricades were moved aside. The limo rolled through and parked at the curb. Rayne peered at the back of the L-shaped courthouse buildings. Beautiful green grass spread in gardens beyond a large porch and steps. On that grass hundreds of reporters and cameramen milled. An enormous bank of microphones stood on the porch, and uniformed police guarded the area. A number of men in shirtsleeves and ties stood on the porch, talking.

Policemen flanked the limo and lined up to escort Rayne and the others to the microphones.

At sight of the car, all reporters' heads turned. Cameras came up. In a mad rush, they jogged toward the limo.

Rayne heard their shouted questions the instant she stepped from the car.

"Rayne, have you heard any more from your daughter?"

"Do you have any idea who kidnapped her?"

"How was she taken from a guarded estate?"

Rayne's heart raced. She was used to crowds, used to paparazzi, but this was too much.

"Is it true you know the vehicle Shaley's in?"

"How are you doing?"

"What about your wedding?"

Rayne's legs felt shaky. No sleep, little food, and all the grief had left her with minimal strength. The crowd sounded so *loud*. Surely the decibels were nothing like the screaming fans at concerts. But every sound pierced her head.

She gripped Gary's hand and walked woodenly between the protective rows of policemen, eyes straight ahead. The sun was overly bright, and her temples thudded. But she would get through this.

Somewhere out there on some TV, maybe Shaley would see her. Would hear the carefully worded sentences meant to send her a message — *we know you didn't mean what you said on the phone.*

Cameras whirred and snapped as reporters crowded against the policemen. Al held Rayne's left elbow, propelling her quickly to the courthouse porch. In his left hand he carried notes. They hurried up the stone steps. Al nudged them back from the microphones. "I'll start, as we planned." His dark eyes studied Rayne's face. In them she read compassion and understanding. Once upon a time, Al and his wife had been through this very same thing. "You all right?" he asked.

No.

Rayne nodded.

Al conferred with his colleagues. A tall, rotund man held the blown-up photo of Shaley. The sight of that beautiful face pierced

Rayne's soul. She gazed at it, then tore her eyes away. Her focus landed on a second man, holding another large poster. Rayne could only see the back, but she knew what it was. Ronald Fledger's despicable face.

"Okay, we're ready." Al exchanged a glance with Gary and walked to the microphone.

The mass of people fell silent. Pens readied against notebooks.

With trembling fingers, Rayne opened her purse and took out the two speeches. She handed Gary's to him. They weren't supposed to read them, and both had memorized every word. But at the moment Rayne didn't know if she could recall even the first sentence. Fuzziness draped her mind. Would her tongue even work?

"Good morning." Al's voice boomed over the microphones. He thanked everyone for coming, then turned and held out an arm toward her and Gary.

Rayne moved toward the microphone bank on someone else's legs. Her entire body started to shake. Cold grief and rage washed over her. Shaley's kidnapper could be watching right now. Suddenly she didn't want to just plead. She wanted to yell and scream, *demand* that he let her daughter go. She wanted to promise she would tear his eyes out, his heart. Pursue him until she died.

A panicked sob kicked up her throat. Gary squeezed her arm. "You want me to go first?" he whispered.

Rayne shook her head. She raised her chin and took deep breaths. *Control, Rayne. For Shaley.*

Al stood aside, and Rayne stepped up to the mics.

She gazed at the hundreds of faces before her but registered none of them. In her mind she saw only one face — Shaley's.

Her mouth opened, and the words flowed.

"I'm Rayne O'Connor. Many of you know me as the lead singer for my band, Rayne. Today, I ask you to see me as a mother who is grieving at the loss of her only child."

The FBI agent holding Shaley's picture moved close to Rayne and held it high.

"This is our daughter, Shaley." Rayne extended her arm toward the poster. "Minutes before Shaley's father and I" — Rayne gestured toward Gary — "were to be married, our daughter was taken from us. Imagine the shock. A wedding turned to anguish."

Rayne's throat tightened. Her fingers curled around the folded paper in her hand.

"We ask the person or people who have Shaley to let her go. We know she wants to come home. *We* want her to come home. Just let her go. Please. We *need* her with us, with her family. We aren't the same without her. We can never be the same. Shaley makes our family whole. She is our — "

Tears stung Rayne's eyes. She clamped down her jaw and blinked rapidly. In her mind she envisioned the multitude of cameras honing in for the tightest shot, drawn to her grief like flies to honey. Fine. If her tears helped Shaley, that's all that mattered.

"She is our joy." Rayne swallowed hard. "We beg you to give her back to us. That is all we want from you."

The words ran out. Had she written more? Rayne looked at Gary, who gave her a reassuring nod — *Good job.*

Rayne stepped to the side, and Gary moved to take her place. The agent holding Shaley's poster moved a few feet to his right, keeping the poster held high.

"I'm Gary Donovon." Gary's voice sounded raw. "Unless you live on another planet, you all know the story of how I reentered Shaley's and Rayne's lives last year."

The reporters near the front smiled wanly.

"Being a father to Shaley, seeing her every day — that was my lifelong dream. That dream came true when I found Rayne and Shaley. Whoever has taken her — please return her to us. We're her family. This is where she belongs."

He stopped. Gulped a breath.

"Today Rayne and I are offering a one-hundred-thousand-dollar reward for Shaley's safe return. If you have any information on where she might be, please contact the authorities. Agent Al Scarrow will give you the number in a minute." Rayne saw Gary look straight into the camera directly in front of him, as if he were facing the kidnapper himself. "Let her go. Now. *Please.* So many people are looking for her. So many want to see her returned to us. We can forget all of this if you'll just let her come back to us." Gary started to say more, then stopped. His head dipped once. "Thank you." He stepped back.

Immediate questions hurled at them.

"Rayne, have you ..."

"Gary, did you ..."

"Do you know ..."

"When ..."

The voices drowned out each other. Al moved up front and raised his hands, signaling quiet.

Policemen gestured for Rayne and Gary to head for the stairs. In no time they were surrounded by escorts. They hustled down the steps, reporters still shouting questions.

"Folks, let me give you important facts that we know." Al's voice boomed over the microphones, but many weren't listening. Rayne picked up her speed. Soon she was running. Who *cared* about a shot of her getting to the limo? Al's information was *important.* The sooner they got out of here, the sooner reporters would listen to the agent.

An eternity passed before they reached the limo. Their driver held the door open. Rayne jumped inside, followed by Gary. The chauffeur shut the door and ran to the driver's side.

Rayne fell into a seat. "Go!" She waved a frantic hand at the chauffeur. "Go!"

As the limo pulled from the curb, Rayne could hear Al's voice spilling into the gardens. "Shaley and Ronald Fledger were last known to be in a cabin outside Provo, Utah. Before that they were filmed by security cameras at a gas station. Shaley was wearing a man's white T-shirt and jeans. Her hair was up in a baseball cap that has *San Diego* written on the front. They were driving a 1997 blue Ford Explorer, license plate ..."

31

The dashboard clock read 11:15. Over two hours since we'd left the gas station.

My stomach rumbled and groaned. I now hadn't eaten for almost twenty-four hours.

The never-ending road stretched before us. Instead of continuing on Highway 20, Joshua had taken every little back road he could, still aiming north. I had the sense we weren't getting very far very fast. I watched signs for towns approaching ... only for us to drive through them without stopping. Joshua now slumped over the steering wheel, grim determination working his jaw. His exhaustion only made him meaner. I didn't dare say anything out of line.

Mostly I said nothing at all.

But one thing was bothering me — a question I couldn't answer. When the time was right, I'd ask Joshua.

At some point we found ourselves back on Highway 20. A new sign read *Ashton — five miles*.

An angry sigh heaved from Joshua. "You're not much company."

"Sorry."

He reached out and turned on the radio. Commercials. I half listened to ads for a car dealership, an insurance company, a bank. Then news came on — and I heard my name.

My muscles stiffened. I wanted to hear that people were looking for me — and I also hoped I didn't. Because who knew how Joshua would react?

His chin bounced up at the news story. He turned the volume higher.

"... the daughter of rock singer Rayne O'Connor," the news announcer said. "This morning on courthouse steps in Santa Barbara, Ms. O'Connor and Shaley's father, Gary Donovon, held a press conference, aided by the FBI and local law enforcement. Shaley was last seen wearing jeans and a plain white T-shirt."

How do they know that?

Joshua's head snapped toward the radio.

"Shaley and her captor were traveling in a 1997 blue Ford Explorer, California license plate 2ZRY394."

A chilling smile spread across Joshua's face.

I pressed back against my seat, rocks in my lungs.

"If you see this vehicle, please call nine-one-one immediately — "

Joshua laughed and slapped off the dial.

I stared straight ahead, new desperation seeping through my chest. What was the point of my planning, of looking for a way to escape? Joshua would never let me out of his sight, and no one would ever find me.

No one.

I wanted to scream and cry. Fingers curling into my palms, I bit my lip and turned toward my window, fighting to hold it together.

"See how smart I am?" Joshua gloated. "Always one step ahead of 'em."

My eyes stung.

"That's the best news I've heard all day." He bounced a fist against the steering wheel. "We got time now. And we ain't got to hide on these little highways all the way to Montana. I'm going to find somewhere to crash for a while. Then we'll hit the freeway and head straight home."

Home. I shuddered. Once we reached his place in the wilderness of Montana, I would have no chance of escape.

I forced my voice to stay even. "Where are we going to stop?" Not that it mattered. Nothing mattered now.

"You just watch."

We reached Ashton. Joshua turned onto Highway 47, much smaller than 20. Bruised hands pressed between my legs, I sat like a statue. My wrists still burned, and my left cheek began to throb. My body was *so* tired. I craved sleep but didn't dare close my eyes. Even when we stopped I couldn't allow myself to sleep. I had to keep my eyes on Joshua every minute.

Where was he going to stop out here?

The highway led us through farmland on the right, skirting a mountain and trees to our left. Few cars passed us.

After rolling through a tiny town named Warm River, the highway climbed into the mountains and forest.

I swallowed. Dared to ask my question again. "Where are we going?"

"To find a cabin." Joshua sounded more energetic just knowing he'd be able to rest soon. "Bound to find a summer getaway out here somewhere. We'll sleep, maybe find something to eat." He gave me a hard look. "And I'll make sure there's no working phone."

"I won't do anything like that again."

"Of course you won't. If you know what's good for you."

What was the point of even trying to get away? I didn't have the strength.

Up ahead I saw a small road leading off 47 to the right. Joshua slowed and turned onto it. "Let's see what we can find."

Nothing, that's what. Trees and more trees. No one around for miles.

And then — a small dirt road. Joshua took it. The road wound through the forest and ended at a wide beige trailer on cinderblocks. No car in sight.

Joshua grunted with satisfaction and pulled up to the place. He stopped the car by yanking on one of the wires he'd rigged. Then he withdrew the gun beneath his seat. "Stay here."

I eyed the weapon, my pulse faltering. What if someone was here? "Please don't kill anybody."

He gave me a long, penetrating look. I saw wildness in his eyes. "'Vengeance is mine,' saith the Lord."

Oh, sure, this was God's doing. And vengeance for what? Happening to be in your own trailer when a madman came knocking?

My mouth went dry.

He slid from the car and walked on stiff legs to the two metal front steps. I watched without moving, a fist pressed to my mouth. Joshua rapped on the door with the butt of the gun.

No answer. He knocked again.

Joshua stuck the gun in the waistband of his pants and grabbed the black step railing. Swung his right leg back and kicked the door with all his might. The door crunched open.

He turned around and gestured for me to get out of the car. Like a beaten puppet, I did as I was told.

Joshua pulled the door back on its broken hinges and motioned for me to go inside first. I stepped into a dim living room smelling of closed-in air and faintly of Lysol. Everything looked clean and cozy. Bright. Like a woman had decorated it. The sofa and matching chair were red, accented with flowered pillows. Magazines were stacked neatly on a rectangular wooden coffee table, and paperbacks filled a tall bookshelf. The cover on the top magazine showed a man fishing. Maybe a couple owned the trailer? To my left sat a small dining table, separating the room from the kitchen. The counters were wiped down, a coffee machine and toaster upon them. Beyond the kitchen stretched a hallway.

"Sit." Joshua gestured to the couch. As I obeyed he ventured down the hall, peering in doors. He returned, looking satisfied. "No phone."

No TV or radio that I could see either. This was a place for someone who just wanted to get away. Indignation for the owners twinged inside me. They didn't deserve this.

Joshua opened the refrigerator door. I strained to look around him, seeing little food on the shelves. No milk, which would spoil quickly. Didn't look like the owners planned to return soon.

How long until they could find a clue from me?

I blinked, pierced by my own question. Even in my despair, even knowing I'd never be rescued, I wasn't ready to give up.

I *had* to keep fighting.

Joshua rummaged around in the refrigerator drawers. "There's bread in here. And cheese and salami." He started pulling out items and laying them on the counter. "Not the Ritz, but we won't starve."

Like he knew anything about the Ritz.

My stomach growled.

I curled my fingers into my legs and surveyed Joshua's back, remembering my fear in the cabin. (Was that days ago?) What would Joshua do to me here?

Quickly I pushed up from the couch. "Want me to make you a sandwich?"

"Sure, fine." He picked up a bottle from the refrigerator door. "Here's some mayonnaise. You need to eat too."

I moved into the kitchen and opened drawers, looking for a knife. Took down two small plates from a cabinet. "Would you check the bedroom closet for me? I still need shoes."

Joshua eyed me again, jaw moving from side to side. "You can't lie to me. I know when you're lying."

I busied myself with opening the mayonnaise jar, spreading the sauce on two slices of bread.

"You *hear* me?"

I raised my gaze to his, forcing myself to look calm. My ankles felt weak. "Yes."

His eyes narrowed. Then he swerved past me and down the hall. I heard the sound of a door opening, soft thuds on the floor of the next room. A moment later Joshua's footsteps headed out of that room and farther down the hall.

My hands placed salami slices on the bread, followed by cheese. Hungry as I was, I hadn't thought I could eat. Now I could barely wait.

An idea popped into my head. I turned and looked at the magazines on the living room coffee table.

Joshua returned, holding a pair of pale blue sneakers and a ladies' green polo shirt. "How about these?" He held out the shoes to me.

I took them, checked inside one for its size. None to be found. "They look about right. Thanks." I set them on the counter.

He nodded. "I'll buy you shoes when we get to Montana, you know. I will take care of you."

I gave him a tight smile.

"And your dress is beautiful."

"Dress?"

"Your wedding dress. It's white with lace. I think I got the right size." His expression creased into anticipation, as if he wanted to please me. As if he really thought this would make me happy.

Fresh dread uncoiled in my stomach. For a moment words stuck in my throat. "A wedding? Who'd be there?"

"Just us and Caleb. And God."

"Don't you need a preacher to marry someone?"

"The marriage will be in God's eyes. That's all that counts."

I licked my lips. "When is this supposed to take place?"

"Not 'supposed to.' *Will*." His mouth spread into a leer. "Soon as we get home."

No. "How long a drive is it from here?"

Joshua pulled down the corners of his mouth. "Now that we can get back on the freeway, maybe a little over nine hours, not counting stops."

Nine hours. Once we left the trailer, I'd have so little time. Sickness rolled through my stomach. "Where in Montana?"

"Why you want to know?"

"Can't I at least know where I'm going to live?"

He tightened his mouth and surveyed me. "Up north. Not far from the Canadian border."

I knew that much already. "What's the nearest town?"

"Stop asking questions!"

I turned back to the sandwiches. The smell of salami now sickened my stomach. I laid the second pieces of bread on top of each sand-wich. Held Joshua's plate out to him. "Here."

"Put this on." He thrust the green shirt in my other hand, then took the plate.

I looked down at the plain white T-shirt he'd given me to wear and remembered the news on the radio. My description had me wearing that shirt. Joshua wasn't taking any chances.

Wordlessly, I picked up the shoes and headed down the hall.

Within twenty-four hours I would be "married" to this monster. The thought weakened my knees.

Behind the locked door of the bathroom I changed shirts. I tried to avoid the mirror, but my gaze drifted to my reflection. I stilled, staring at my face as I'd never seen it. My left eye wasn't as puffy, but the bruising had turned purple black. The color matched the bruises on my arms and hands. My hair straggled from the rub-ber band I'd used to make a ponytail. Everything about me looked beaten and worn, like I was twenty years older. My face reminded me of pictures of battered women.

You are *battered, Shaley. Welcome to your new life.*

I turned away from the mirror and stared at the white T-shirt I'd dropped on the floor.

A voice inside my head told me to pick it up.

I draped it over my arm and looked back to the mirror. It was a cover to a medicine cabinet. I opened it up.

On the clear shelves inside I saw a box of Band-Aids, a bottle of aspirin, two toothbrushes and toothpaste, and various hand and face creams. On the top shelf—a tube of lipstick and an eyebrow pencil.

I picked up the eyebrow pencil and took off the top to examine the point. It was sharp enough to write with.

Clutching the pencil, I sat on the closed toilet, listening to the rapid beat of my heart. I could leave this shirt behind. If I only knew exactly where we were headed.

But I *did* remember the license plate of our new car.

I knelt on the floor and spread out the shirt. Poised the pencil to write — then straightened.

No. There was a better way.

I pulled my bottom lip between my teeth. This plan was much more of a gamble. If Joshua caught me, he'd beat the rest of me black and blue. Then kill me.

My eyes squeezed shut. Did I dare?

What choice did I have?

Leaning over once again, I turned the shirt lengthwise and began to write in large block letters.

A banging hit the door. My body jerked.

"What're you doing in there?"

I swallowed. "Changing clothes."

"Can't take that long."

"Joshua, where do you think I can go from here — float up through the ceiling?" The window was hardly big enough for me to get through.

He growled. "Get *out* of there."

"Coming."

I batted at the toilet paper holder, purposely making noise. Then flushed the toilet. Turned the water on in the sink. With shaking hands I bent down to finish my writing task. Done, I lifted the shirt and held it up toward the window, checking to see if the light made the lettering visible from the front of the shirt.

It didn't.

I folded the T-shirt lengthwise, writing inside, and placed the eyebrow pencil upon it. Rolled up the shirt.

"Sha —"

"There's lipstick in the medicine cabinet. Can I keep it?"

"You ain't gonna be wearin' no lipstick."

I picked up the tube and plunked it back down on the shelf hard enough to make a *click*. Closed the medicine cabinet.

Holding the rolled-up T-shirt casually by my side, I opened the bathroom door. Joshua's gaze fell to the shirt.

I managed a shrug. "I want to take it with me. Use it as a pillow in the car."

He lifted a shoulder. Weariness dragged at his face. "I got to get some sleep. You take the back bedroom. I'll take this front one. Doors stay open, and I'm a light sleeper. You ain't gonna get past me down this hall, so no use trying."

"Where would I go? There's no one around here for miles."

"Get back in the bedroom."

"Can I get some of those books and magazines up there first?" I gestured toward the living room. "Or let me just stay up there. I haven't eaten my sandwich yet."

His eyes narrowed. Swiveling on his heel, he stomped up the hall. I snatched the pair of shoes from the floor and followed some distance behind him. In the living room Joshua pulled the front door shut as best as it would go. The hinges groaned. He opened it again, experimenting. More squeaks and moans. He banged it closed.

"Fine. Stay up here. You won't get through that door without waking me up. And if you try, you'll be very, very sorry." He lifted the bottom of his shirt high enough to show me his gun.

"I won't. I just want to eat and read."

Joshua stepped toward me. I melted back into the kitchen and let him pass.

The bed in the first bedroom creaked as he fell upon it.

I stood in the kitchen, clutching the T-shirt and shoes. Afraid to move. Afraid to even ask myself what I dared do now.

32

At twelve thirty in the afternoon, Randy Sullivan dragged himself home. Misery roiled in his gut, despite the pep-talk debriefing from Bear. Every member of the team had felt just as bad — Randy could see it in their faces, the sag of their shoulders. They were rescuers, fighters. *Fixers*. But they hadn't rescued anyone today.

"This wasn't our fault," Bear insisted. "Somehow the HT got through those guys before they even set up a proper roadblock."

Randy knew that. They all did. It didn't help.

He pulled into his garage and cut the engine. Searched inside himself for a smile for his son and wife. Tiredness ragged at him. He needed sleep.

"Daddy, daddy!" Stevie rushed to grab Randy's legs as soon as he entered the kitchen. Rhonda hurried over from the sink.

"Hey, guy." Randy picked up his son and jiggled him high in the air. Stevie laughed. "Whatcha doin'?"

Stevie's cherub face hung above his dad's. "Watching cartoons, and Mom made pancakes."

"Like a heart?"

"Yeah." The boy's eyes sparkled.

"That's great!" Randy plunked Stevie back on his feet and hugged Rhonda. "Hi, lovely."

She clung to him, her face in his neck. "Glad you're back."

He stroked her hair. "Yeah."

Rhonda pulled away and looked at him. "The press conference was on TV. I snuck back in the bedroom to watch."

Randy nodded. He'd called her with the news when they'd returned to the Stable. As much as he tried to keep the remorse from his expression, he knew Rhonda saw it. She always did.

"Your team did what it was supposed to do," she whispered.

"Yeah."

"Randy, don't beat yourself up over this."

"Yeah." But of course he would. His eyes slid to Stevie, who once again hugged his knees. The thought of his own son being snatched from him made his heart stop. How did any parent *survive* that?

Randy managed a little smile and tugged at Rhonda's hair. "Let me sleep for a few hours?"

"You've earned it."

Five minutes later Randy fell onto the bed, beat and depressed. Sleep would not come. He could only stare at the ceiling, thinking of Shaley. Wondering if she was still alive.

They should have been there in time. They *should* have.

Randy wasn't a praying man, but he sent a message heavenward for this one.

God — if you hear me, let this girl come home.

I sat on the red couch in the trailer's living room, listening to Joshua's snores drifting from the bedroom. He'd fallen onto the bed only minutes ago. I envied him. How I wished I could sleep.

For the rest of my life.

The blue sneakers sat on the floor nearby. I thought it best not to put them on yet. I'd placed the rolled-up T-shirt on the couch to my left.

From my position I could strain my neck and read the clock on the kitchen stove. Just after noon.

My sandwich still sat on the counter. I should eat it. Who knew when I'd get another chance? But now that Joshua was fully asleep, I had more important things to do.

Quietly, I picked up the top magazine from the stack on the coffee table — *The Outdoorsman*. Every movement I made was slow. I was too aware of my clothes rustling, my own breathing. I didn't want to wake Joshua. On the bottom right of the magazine's cover stretched a mailing label. *Ed and Jean Carroll, 1011 West Tryndle, Idaho Falls, 83401.*

I ran my thumb over the names. Ed and Jean. I tried to picture them in their Idaho Falls house. How strange to have this connection. The two of them there, me here in their trailer. Did they feel the violation of their getaway place in their souls?

"Ed and Jean Carroll," I whispered. I would never forget those names.

I set the magazine on the couch to my right. Took hold of the cover just above the mailing label. Slowly, I began to tear off the label, making only a ghost of a sound. When it came away in my hand, I tucked it in the front right pocket of my jeans.

Leaning toward the coffee table, I placed the magazine at the bottom of the stack.

For a long time I stared at the paperbacks on the bookshelf. Finally, with careful movements, I rose and padded toward the books. I took down the first paperback my fingers touched and carried it back to the couch. Then unrolled the T-shirt and picked up the eyebrow pencil. On the inside cover of the book I wrote: *Shaley O'Connor was here Sunday, May 16, 2010. Kidnapped May 15. Joshua is taking me to Montana, near the Canadian border. Please find me!*

Cocking my head toward the bedrooms, I heard Joshua's snoring.

I rolled the eyebrow pencil up in the T-shirt once again. Replaced the book on the shelf. But I left it sticking out a little. Not enough that I thought Joshua would notice. But Jean would. She was that sort of housekeeper.

After some time I managed to eat my sandwich and guzzle a glass of water.

Around one thirty, exhaustion hit. I sat on the couch, staring at the front door. There it stood, mere feet away. All I had to do was yank it open, run outside ...

And go where? I didn't know how to hot-wire the car. And how long could I hide in the woods as Joshua searched for me? Carrying his gun. Even if he didn't find me right away, what would I do when night fell? We were so far from a town, from even another house.

Defeat wrapped cold fingers around my throat. I slumped against the back cushions of the couch, then laid down on my side. Stuck one of the bright, flowered pillows beneath my head. I drew the rolled-up T-shirt close to my chest and hugged it.

Sleepiness washed over me in waves, pulling me down ... down into fitful sleep. Twice I awoke to silence, only to feel my heavy eyelids close again. I dreamt of weddings — Mom and Dad's beautiful ceremony morphing into my own nightmare.

A noise popped my eyes open.

Footsteps.

Down the hall a door closed. Joshua, going into the bathroom.

My arms still clutched the T-shirt. I pushed to a sitting position, eyes pulling toward the paperback on the shelf. It sat just as I left it, sticking out from the other books about an inch.

Straightening, I peered toward the clock on the stove. Eight fifteen. My mouth opened. *Eight fifteen?* I'd been asleep almost seven hours.

The bathroom door opened. I dropped the T-shirt onto the couch.

Joshua came up the hall. I tensed. He sneered at me. "Still here, I see."

My gaze fell to the floor.

"You sleep?" he asked.

"Yeah."

Joshua stretched with satisfaction, tilting his jowly face from side to side. "We need to get going."

Desperation flamed in my chest. *Nine hours.* In darkness. What if we reached the cabin before dawn? My plans for the T-shirt would never work.

I had to delay him.

Casually, I moved the T-shirt to the carpet beneath the coffee table. "Don't you want something to eat first?"

Joshua heaved a sigh and placed both hands on his hips. "Yeah. Might as well. Less stopping on the way."

"I'll get something." I rose from the couch and brushed past him to enter the kitchen. That mere touch made the hair on my arms stand up.

Nine hours.

I opened cabinet doors and found shelves full of canned goods. Soup, baked beans, vegetables. I grabbed a can. "Want some chili?"

He shrugged. "Sure."

I found a pan beneath the stove and poured in the chili. Placed it on a burner over low heat. My eyes wouldn't stop glancing at the clock. Was it *frozen*? The hands were barely moving.

What time would the sun rise?

The smell of chili wafted into the air.

When it started to bubble, I poured it into a bowl and set it on the table with a spoon. "There you go."

"Thanks." He pulled out a chair.

I watched him from the corner of my eye. *Thanks.* First time he'd said anything half nice to me.

My thoughts fled down the corridor of days, months, years. Stuck in some cabin serving this despicable man. I couldn't imagine my life. It simply couldn't be. Fresh disbelief welled up in my chest. I still couldn't grasp this was really happening.

God, please help me!

Joshua ate all too quickly. I went to the bathroom, drank some water. Put on Jean's sneakers. They fit.

I offered to do the dishes.

"No, we're leaving." He wiped his mouth with the back of his hand and pushed from the table.

The clock read 8:33.

"Please. It won't take long. Haven't we done enough to this place, breaking in the door?"

Joshua waved a hand in the air. "Make it quick."

I washed the plates from earlier, as well as the pot and bowl and spoon. Dried them. Left them out on the counter. When Ed and Jean came back, I wanted them to see I'd at least done this for them.

"Let's go." Joshua pointed toward the door.

Nothing else left to do.

Boldly, I walked to the coffee table and picked up a women's magazine. "I want to take this with me." As I leaned over, I plucked the T-shirt off the floor, silently pleading Joshua wouldn't make me leave it behind. Or worse, check it.

My heart fluttered as I straightened. My eyes grazed past Joshua to the stove clock. It was 8:39.

The sun was setting as we drove away.

Another endless night. Brittany didn't know how they'd live through it.

She sat in the great room with Rayne, Ross, Gary, and the band members. Everyone was scattered throughout the room on couches and chairs that had been moved back from the circle.

Agent Scarrow was in the dining room with his files and laptop. Brittany didn't even want to see his face right now. He couldn't seem to give them any good news.

Why hadn't someone spotted the Explorer?

"Maybe he ditched the Explorer for something else." Gary spoke as if he had read Brittany's thoughts. "If everyone heard the press conference, he probably did too. Maybe we shouldn't have told them after all."

"Stop, Gary." Kim pointed at him. "You did the best you could. And besides, the FBI agreed to tell."

Rayne didn't reply. Brittany knew she was just too tired.

In the dining room, Agent Scarrow's phone rang. Brittany stilled. Every call brought fresh hope ... then disappointment. Her head tilted toward the sound of his voice, but she couldn't make out many of his words. A moment later the agent's chair scraped back from the table. His footsteps sounded on the marble floor. When he appeared, everyone in the room focused on him.

Rayne and Gary stood and faced the agent. Brittany sucked in a breath.

Agent Scarrow raised a hand. "The Explorer has been found in a parking lot just south of Salt Lake City. It's been abandoned, apparently for another car."

"Oh." Rayne reached for Gary's arm.

Weakness flooded Brittany. How would they ever find Shaley now?

"So now what?" Ross strode toward Agent Scarrow. Kim, Rich, Morrey, and the rest of the band members left their seats to crowd around.

The Explorer had been discovered in the back parking lot of a strip mall, Agent Scarrow told them. The owner of a maroon Toyota Camry had left her car in that parking lot since morning. When she returned the Camry was gone. She called the police. The responding officer immediately recognized what she'd been too upset to notice — the license plate of the Explorer parked in the very next spot.

"It's a pretty good bet Shaley's now in that Camry," the agent said. "As we speak, a bulletin for the stolen car is going out. We'll have law enforcement everywhere looking for it."

"But the public won't know." Brittany bit the side of her cheek. "They'll still be looking for the Explorer. Plus now it's dark, so how will policemen even see the Camry?"

"Yeah." Morrey rubbed his arms. "But the kidnapper won't know *we* know what car he's in."

"That's right." Agent Scarrow nodded. "He thinks he's eluded us again. Maybe that'll make him sloppy."

"But what if we're wrong?" Gary's voice edged. "What if they're not in the Camry at all?"

"That's a possibility but not likely. The minute the suspect ditched the Explorer, he'd need another car. Since the one right next to that Explorer is now missing, it makes sense to proceed with this lead."

Salt Lake City, Brittany thought. He was taking Shaley farther and farther north.

"What about the Explorer?" Rayne asked. "Will they check it?"

"It's already being towed to the local police station. They'll go over it for fingerprints and other evidence."

Please, God, don't let them find more blood in it!

"Even though it's night now, I want you to know the car will be processed immediately," Agent Scarrow said. "As far as everyone's concerned, there's no off time on this case."

Brittany and the others peppered Agent Scarrow with more questions until there was nothing left to ask. His phone rang again, and he disappeared back into the dining room.

Rayne and Gary wandered out the rear doors of the great room and onto the huge deck overlooking the lighted gardens. Brittany watched them, trying to imagine their wedding that should have been. Yesterday seemed like years ago. All the white rented tents for the reception had been taken down from the backyard. Brittany hadn't even noticed when that happened.

She floated through the next few hours, her mind whirling with fear. Shaley's second night away from them. What was happening to her?

Shortly after eleven o'clock, Agent Scarrow received more news. Some of the band members had wandered off to their bedrooms. Brittany, Rayne, and Gary remained in the great room.

"They've processed the Explorer," Agent Scarrow told them.

Rayne gasped. "Did they find blood?"

"No blood." He gave her a tired smile. "Useable fingerprints were lifted from the steering wheel and driver's door. These match the ones found in the van's driver's area and the pay phone, which we know belong to Ronald Fledger. Techs also found numerous pieces of evidence from Shaley. Two are particularly noteworthy. The first are seven of her hairs. The second is an absolutely perfect thumbprint on the back window on the driver's side. The position of this thumb-print, near the bottom of the window and with no other fingerprints near it, leads us to believe Shaley intentionally put it there."

The information filtered through Brittany, trailing hope. Shaley was fighting back.

"The hairs also look as if Shaley plucked them out and purposely dropped them on the floor of the backseat. The seven hairs were found in a cluster, with follicles attached. Our theory is that Shaley was lying down in that third row of seats. Maybe she knew the kidnapper was going to steal another car. She wanted to leave her mark behind."

"She hasn't given up hope," Rayne whispered.

"I think you're right." Al put a hand on his hip. "This is very good news. It's one thing to find evidence. It's another to find evidence that tells you the mind-set of the victim. Even as we're separated from Shaley, she's leaving a trail. She's trying to connect. That tells us her inner strength and her intelligence. She's doing all she can — right now — to help us find her."

Keep it up, Shaley. Brittany closed her eyes, envisioning her best friend. *Lead us to you.*

I sat in the front passenger seat, watching the road, trying to memorize every sign on the route as our headlights swept over them. The rolled-up T-shirt lay under my seat. Every once in a while, I pushed a sneakered foot against it, just to feel its bulk. Just to know it was still there.

After meandering off the tiny back road that led to the trailer, we'd reconnected with Highway 20 and followed it north, crossing into Montana. It then took us over the border into Wyoming, nearing Yellowstone National Park. Joshua turned north on Highway 191. We crossed back into Montana.

How did he know all these roads? It's like he'd memorized a map.

A question that had bugged me popped back into my mind.

"How did you know about the jewelry van?" I kept my eyes on the road.

"Who's askin'?"

Huh? I glanced at him. He drove with one hand on the steering wheel, his right arm resting on the console. His full lips worked, and his beady eyes focused on the road with hunger, as if one more mile under our wheels meant one mile closer to "home."

"*I'm* asking."

He threw me a look. "The old Shaley, or the new Joshua's girl Shaley?"

I forced myself not to grimace. I would *never* be "Joshua's girl."

"You obviously planned this really well. I can't figure out how you did it, that's all."

He chuckled, a dry rasp in his throat. "You think about it some more."

I watched our headlights eat up the road, obstinacy festering within me. I didn't want to figure this out. I wanted to persuade Joshua to tell me. The more he talked, the more lax he might become. Maybe I'd hear something really useful, beyond satisfying my curiosity.

An eternal half hour passed. I lifted my hands. "Tell me about the van."

"You can't figure it out?"

"No."

He grunted. "Must not be as smart as I thought."

"Guess not."

Joshua drew a long breath. "I've been planning this a long time. Just didn't know when or how. Then God dropped the perfect opportunity into my lap."

God? How *dare* this kidnapper, this *criminal*, credit God for this! I stared through the windshield, jaw tightening. The God I worshiped didn't lead people to evil; he led them toward good. If Joshua didn't know that, he was crazy.

Or merely rationalizing.

My shoulders sagged. How sad to think not everyone who called on God did it righteously. It made figuring out this world all the harder.

I pushed back the emotions, made sure my voice would sound even. "How did he do that?"

"You know that jeweler down by where you live? The one that did the rings? I know the security guy there, works at night. He told me he'd heard from an employee that the man's ring didn't fit when it was delivered."

That would have been Friday. Not much time for planning.

"My friend said Rayne called the store and got all huffy. Said there was no time for them to fix it."

I bit back a retort. It *was* a sloppy mistake. Mom had been upset, but I'd been even more furious.

"I asked him what they were gonna do. He'd heard that Rayne said she'd have to get a jeweler in Santa Barbara to resize it."

Once more, I fought to keep my expression placid. To think this horror was all because of that mistake. "So you started checking out jewelry stores there?"

Joshua snorted. "Santa Barbara ain't that big a town. It's not like your fancy cars rolled in with nobody noticin'. I hung around downtown, dressed up fine to blend in. When I saw one of those limos stop at a jewelry store — that was it. I went into the store, pretending to look at watches. Heard one of them big muscle guys of yours — the one with the black hair sticking straight up — talking to the jeweler. Muscle Man said the ring had to be delivered before the ceremony and given to you personally. He gave exact orders where the van should go."

I looked at my lap. Wendell had only been following my orders. I was so ticked about that ring I didn't want anyone else handling it. "What if he hadn't told the jeweler to deliver the ring only to me?"

Joshua cast me a long look. "Then you wouldn't be sittin' here, would you."

My nerves prickled. It was too much to take in. My own anger and forcefulness over that ring had led to *this*? What if I'd kept my cool?

What if the ring had fit? What if Joshua hadn't known that security guard?

I laced my bruised hands to keep them from shaking. So many little things added up to make this happen. The lack of any one of them could have derailed it.

Joshua laughed. "All I had to do was lie in wait for that van. I stashed the other car in the meantime, knowing we'd have to change over quickly." He waggled his head back and forth, as if immensely pleased with himself.

How I wanted to say, *I know who you are, Joshua! You're no prophet, you're just a criminal who used to stalk me.*

I could not live the rest of my life with this man. As his *wife*. I *couldn't.* New, clawing panic gripped me, curling my fingers into my palms. I had mere hours left, almost all of them in darkness. Even if somehow the police knew about the Camry, who would see the license plate at night on this nearly deserted highway?

The clock read 11:31. Despair descended over me. Every mile took me closer to my fate.

Just past midnight we hit Bozeman, Montana.

"We'll stop for gas here." Joshua aimed me a chilling smile. "And this is where we hit the freeway for a while. All the quicker to get us home."

PART 3
Monday

The night wore on, my defiant hope fading with each mile. We drove on Interstate 90 for less than an hour, the night hiding me from any eyes that may have recognized me, that may have helped. I thought of the evidence I'd left in the Explorer and knew that it was all for nothing. Of the book in the trailer, in which I'd written my name and a note. Why had I even thought that would help? I didn't know the name of the town close to Joshua's cabin, and Montana was a huge state. Police could search for years and not find me. I knew Mom and Dad would never give up. But the imaginings of what would happen to me for months ... years as they searched dried up my heart.

I sat in the Camry's passenger seat, beyond numb. Part of my mind refused to believe I even existed anymore. I was a shell of a body hurtling through darkness. No way out for me. No help. No hope.

God, where are you?

Joshua no longer tried to get me to talk. With every minute he sat straighter. As if it didn't matter now what I did, trapped in this car while he drove. What mattered was when we got "home." When he would make me do whatever he liked, and no one would be close enough to hear my cries.

I couldn't look at him, not even a glance. In my mind he grew uglier and more contemptible as the hours ticked by.

At a town called Big Timber, we turned off the freeway onto Highway 191. It ran through the small, dead town, then crossed railroad tracks and a river. After that — north into more nothingness.

Sometimes I stared dully at the deserted road. Sometimes I closed my eyes and imagined Mom and Dad's wedding. By now they would have been on their honeymoon at a quiet resort in the Fiji islands. Brittany, the band, and I would have been back home in Southern California. How far away that all seemed now. Like a dream. Like someone else's life.

We hit another town. Lewistown. I barely noticed the sign. What did it matter anyway? We'd drive through here and be gone, no trace of me left behind.

Joshua turned off Highway 191 onto some smaller road. "Heading east," he said, as if I cared. Then it hit me. I'd thought he was taking me north toward Canada. Maybe he'd lied. Which meant my note in that paperback in Ed and Jean's trailer would only send searchers in the wrong direction.

With that realization, the last bit of fight in me died.

Around four thirty in the morning, the first streaks of light shimmered across the sky and through the front windshield. Dawn was coming. The first day in my new life.

Fear seeped through me until my limbs felt useless.

We were still headed east.

I pressed my foot against the balled-up T-shirt under my seat. Such hopes I'd had for that shirt. Now it would be no help at all.

"We'll turn before too long." Joshua was wide awake, the fingers of his right hand drumming against the steering wheel. "North. After that it's only about an hour."

North. The word echoed in my head. *North.*

A tiny flame sparked within me.

"What's the name of the town?" I asked.

"Told you, we're not livin' in a town."

"But you said one's close. What is it?"

He turned to me, a leering grin on his face. "Peace. Peace, Montana."

I glanced at him, then looked away. "You're making that up."

"Nope. That's the name."

Peace. Didn't that just fit. About as misnamed as Joshua's being a "prophet."

I watched the sun peep over the horizon directly ahead of us. Never had I seen such a depressing sight. Joshua and I put down our visors, but it didn't help. The sun was still too low.

Everywhere I looked I saw emptiness. The landscape was mostly barren hills with scattered scruffy trees. This world was vast and dry. I couldn't imagine living in it.

At five fifty Joshua slowed and turned left onto an even smaller road. "Just one hour to go," he gloated.

The newly risen sun shone into my window.

I moved the heel of my right foot back and forth, rubbing against the T-shirt. Here was my chance. I could use it now after all. There was only one problem: not one person was around to see it.

I slumped down in my seat, thinking, *What's the use?* I might as well show the T-shirt to Joshua, admit my "sin," and plead for forgiveness before he found it. Maybe that way he would hit me less.

Peace, a voice in my head whispered. *Peace, Montana.*

Maybe we would drive through the town.

I pulled in a breath and held it. That tiny flame I'd felt a while back flickered a little higher. Maybe I still had a chance.

The sun warmed the right side of my face.

I made a point of squinting. Turned my head slightly toward Joshua, away from the brightness. One hand came up, shielding my eyes.

My heart fluttered into a double-time beat. Did I dare try this?

If it went wrong, Joshua would beat me for sure. He'd pull the car over right on the road, and who'd be around to stop him? Maybe he'd get mad enough to strangle me.

I breathed deeply but quietly, trying to hide my fear.

The sun rose higher. More heat, more brightness. Before I could stop myself, I leaned over. Pulled the T-shirt out from under the seat.

"I'm going to put this in my window." Did I sound normal? Did my voice betray me? My legs trembled. "So the sun's not in my eyes."

Joshua merely grunted.

Here goes nothing.

I had to unroll the shirt without allowing Joshua to see the writing on it. Suddenly I realized that was impossible.

And — *oh, no.* That eyebrow pencil was still inside the shirt. Why had I put it back like that? I should have shoved it under the couch in the trailer.

For a second I froze, heart clicking like a train going down a track. I should have thought this through better.

There had to be a way.

I put down my window an inch. Fresh, cool air blew over me. Turning away from Joshua, I unrolled the T-shirt until the eyebrow pencil came into view. With my right hand I pulled out the pencil and dropped it between my seat and the front door.

No reaction from Joshua. He hadn't seen it.

I unrolled the T-shirt the rest of the way, until it remained merely folded in half lengthwise. My writing was inside that fold. With thumb and forefinger at each end of the fabric, I lifted the top fold, raised the shirt to the window, and draped it over the glass.

When I let go with one hand to close the window, wind blew the shirt down. It flipped over, exposing some of the writing.

I shot Joshua a frantic sideways glance. His eyes were on the road, a smile on his face.

Pulse racing, I snatched up the shirt. Tried again. The wind blew it off the glass a second time. Panic swept through me.

"You might as well forget that." Joshua sounded amused.

"I don't like the sun in my eyes." Surely he heard how breathy my voice was. Surely he saw how I shook.

With clumsy fingers I rolled up the window a little until I could barely force the fabric through the opening. When the shirt was in place, I took away my left hand and slid my right hand all the way across the window, using my forearm and elbow to hold the T-shirt steady. Quickly, I hit the button to roll up the window. The T-shirt caught.

I pressed back in my seat, trying to steady my breathing. Shot Joshua a glance. He drove on, unconcerned.

Because of the curve of the car, the end of the T-shirt hung an inch or two out from the bottom of the window. Would that make it harder to read the words on the other side? I rested my arm on the sill, forcing the shirt toward the glass.

Long minutes passed before my heartbeat began to slow.

After a while my arm started to go to sleep. I brought it down. No people around us now anyway. If we drove through Peace, I'd rest my arm on the sill again.

If we drove through the town. *Please, God, let us do that.* How could anyone not help after seeing the message on that T-shirt? In big block letters I'd written:

HELP! I'M SHALEY. KIDNAPPED!

Dawn.

Rayne walked the floor of her bedroom, every inch of her weighted with tiredness and grief. A second night with no sleep. Another day to face.

Why had no one spotted that Camry? It was as if Shaley and her kidnapper had dropped off the face of the earth. Were they holed up somewhere? Had that despicable man realized his mistake in stealing the Camry and ditched it for yet another car? What if he hadn't stolen that Camry at all, and police were looking for the wrong vehicle?

So many questions.

Some minutes Shaley felt so close to Rayne — as if she could reach out and touch her daughter. As if, even separated, their hearts beat as one. Moments later Rayne would feel the miles between them as big as the galaxy.

She could not go on like this.

Rayne's legs weakened. Sinking to her knees by the bed, she begged God to save her daughter.

An odd thing happened as the prayers poured out. A quieting seeped into her soul. For the first time since Shaley had gone missing, Rayne found herself not demanding *Why?* Instead came the thought — *God, how could I have lived through the last day and a half without you?*

The prayers trickled away, followed by tears. Rayne slipped off her knees to lie in a fetal position. She sobbed weakly, breath hitching, wetness rolling toward her left cheek and onto the carpet. She cried until she could cry no more ... then drifted into fitful sleep.

The next thing she knew, someone was knocking on her door. "Rayne? Rayne."

She pushed herself to a sitting position, groggy and disoriented. "Yeah."

"It's Al. I have some news."

For fifteen minutes after I'd hung the T-shirt in my window, I sat without speaking. But inside my head was anything but silence. Prayers wailed through my mind, begging God for the chance to drive through Peace, for rescue. As our wheels ate up the miles, I *felt* the nearing presence of our new "home." It felt dark and oppressive. Might as well have been a dungeon instead of some cabin in the wilderness. Loathing and despair crept through me. I could not arrive there. Live there.

Then, like a desert mirage, I spotted buildings down the road. My heart leapt into my throat. "Is that Peace?"

"Yup."

My right hand dropped down to feel the eyebrow pencil lying by my door. I pushed it beneath my seat.

For a moment I couldn't form a sound.

"Nice town." Joshua sounded proud, as if he'd founded the place himself. "People leave you alone."

No. Don't leave us alone!

"How many people live there?" I forced casualness into my tone.

"I don't know. Couple thousand, maybe." Joshua gave me a hard look. "Not that you'll be making friends there."

I swallowed. The town grew closer.

With a deep breath, I shifted in my seat and lifted my right arm to lie against the window.

I checked the clock. It was still so early in the morning. Peering through the windshield, I saw no one as we approached the town. Surely someone had to be awake and on the streets. *Please, God.*

At the edge of town we passed a sign. *Peace. Population: 1,882.* The speed limit dropped to thirty. Joshua slowed to forty.

My heart knocked against my ribs. I licked my lips, concentrating on resting my left hand on my knee, fingers open. They wanted to clench. To shake. They wanted to pound against the windshield and yell for someone to notice me.

We crossed into the town. Small wood houses lined each side of the street, giving way to businesses. A small grocery, a hardware store. The road became Main Street, with dilapidated storefronts, some empty. Not one was open yet.

Anxiety pressed my lungs until I could barely breathe. Just three blocks ahead, I could see open road again. So little time for anyone to appear.

We rolled through the next block, my eyes darting left and right. Still I saw no one. Panic clawed at my windpipe. I pressed the backs of my legs against my seat to keep them from trembling.

We hit another block. Only one remained. The town sat silent and empty. A crazy thought struck me — that Joshua knew all about my T-shirt and somehow had come here ahead of time, killing everyone so we could roll through, undisturbed. I threw him a glance. He turned his head and leered.

"Not far now." He chuckled low in his throat. "I did it. I really did it."

Here it came — the final block. Nothing but open country, brown and hilly, beyond it. I wanted to cry. I wanted to scream. I wanted to shove open my door and fling myself onto the pavement. What if I did? Would someone hear me before Joshua forced me back into the car? What price would I pay?

We neared the edge of town. It was now or never. My muscles gathered, energy pooling. My limbs tensed, ready to spring —

Joshua grunted in disgust. My eyes jerked to him. He was looking in the rearview mirror. My right arm came off the window. I started to turn.

"Stop!" he barked. "You just look straight ahead."

"What is it?"

"Police car."

A second passed before my chaotic mind could register. *Police? Where had he come from?*

Joshua flicked another look into the mirror. "Nothin' to worry about." Joshua's words were clipped, tense. "He just happened to turn onto the street behind us."

A coincidence, that was all. We hadn't passed a police car on my side of the Camry, I was sure of that. No way he could have seen the T-shirt. No way.

"Don't you move." Joshua's voice darkened with threat. "Don't forget I got that gun under my seat. Wouldn't want you to make me have to kill him."

I stared straight ahead, eyes burning.

The town faded past us. I fought to keep my chin up, my mouth from trembling.

Joshua continued to glance in the rearview mirror. He leaned toward the steering wheel, his back not touching the seat.

"Is he still there?" I whispered.

No reply. Left hand on the wheel, Joshua bent down and fished underneath the seat with his right hand. He brought up the gun. Laid it in his lap.

My stomach fluttered. "Don't hurt him. Please. He can't know anything."

Behind us a siren whooped once.

My breath sucked in. I turned wide eyes to Joshua. His face blackened. Curses spilled from his lips.

"What are you — "

"Shut up!"

The siren whooped again. I saw a flash of red reflected in the mirror.

No, policeman, go away. Don't stop us!

Joshua reached over and dug his fingers into my thigh. I gasped in pain. "*Don't* you move," he seethed. "Don't say a word. You hear?"

"Please don't shoot him."

"*Do you hear?*"

"Yes. Yes!"

Joshua slowed the car and pulled toward the side of the road. We stopped.

Fear cocooned me. I couldn't move. I watched Joshua as from some distant place as he left the car in drive, put his foot on the brake. With his left hand he hit the button to roll down his window. His right hand picked up the gun and held it low, down by the front of his seat.

Footsteps sounded on pavement. They grew closer. I couldn't just sit there and let this policeman *die*.

Joshua's fingers gripped his weapon, knuckles whitening.

The officer reached Joshua's window. Leaned down.

"No!" I screamed. "Run!"

The officer's surprised eyes locked with mine. Joshua's right arm rose. The policeman jerked back. My hand shot out and punched Joshua's elbow — just as he pulled the trigger. His aim went wild out the window. The policeman grabbed for his gun, yanked it out.

Joshua re-aimed.

"No!" I hit him again — too late.

He fired. A bullet hole punched in the officer's right chest. The man grunted and staggered back. Sank to his knees, then fell face forward.

I froze, sick to the core. Hot tears sprang to my eyes.

"You're dead now, Shaley, you're *dead!*" Joshua smacked his foot on the accelerator. We jolted forward, throwing me back against my seat. Tires squealing, he peeled out onto the highway, leaving the dying policeman in the dust.

40

Rayne swayed to her feet and crossed the bedroom. She flung open the door to see Al, with Gary close behind. Gary surged past the FBI agent. "They've seen Shaley! They've *seen Shaley*!" He grabbed Rayne by the shoulders and hung on. But his face showed only terror.

Rayne's eyes widened. Her head swiveled from Gary to Al. "Where? What happened? How is she?"

"In Montana." Gary's words spilled over themselves. "Near the Canadian border. A policeman stopped their car and ..." His face whitened. He shook his head at Al. "Tell her."

Al held up a hand, palm out — his gesture for Rayne to stay calm. "It's in a little town called Peace, Montana. They're in the stolen Camry, just as we suspected. An officer pulled them over on a routine stop for exceeding the speed limit. He hadn't seen the Be on the Lookout for the car and had no idea what he was walking into."

"Did he get Shaley?" Rayne blurted. Her lungs felt on fire. "Is she safe?"

"I'm afraid it didn't happen that way. Fledger shot him and took off."

"No." The heat in Rayne's chest spread through her body. "Is he dead? Is Shaley ..."

"Looks like the officer will pull through. He was shot in the upper right chest, so it missed his heart. He was able to drag himself back to his car and radio for help. Local police vehicles are on their way. There's only one road leading out of that town for some distance.

State police have also been alerted. They're putting a chopper in the air."

Rayne clutched Gary's hands, her nerves zinging with hope and fear. What if Fledger shot Shaley? What if he drove so fast he crashed the car? "What do we do now?" she whispered. "What do we *do*?"

"We pray." Gary squeezed her hands until it hurt. His handsome face looked worn and old, his eyes red. "We pray."

41

I pressed against my seat, hands clutched in my lap and tears rolling down my face. The sight of the policeman collapsing on the road flashed again and again in my head. It was all my fault. Maybe he *had* seen the T-shirt in the window. He'd come to help me — and now he was dead.

Joshua drove like a wild man, hunched over the wheel and cursing. We sped past rocky hills on the straight road. With every mile I knew we would wreck.

Maybe it would be better that way. Just crash and die. Anything was better than what awaited me.

Joshua glanced in the rearview mirror and spat another curse. I resisted the urge to turn around and look. Instead I lowered my visor and peered into the attached mirror.

Flashing red lights — far back in the distance.

All air sucked from my lungs. New, wild hope surged through me, pursued by terror. I could die here.

Joshua gunned the motor. Our speed hit ninety-five. He gripped the steering wheel, teeth clenched. His breath came in hard puffs. "I'm *not* lettin' them take you."

I watched the road fly at us, my muscles stiff as wood.

"Take that T-shirt off the window," Joshua spat. "I need to see."

Quickly I rolled the window down an inch, yanked down the shirt, and stuffed it under my seat. Closed the window again.

A minute passed. Two. My eyes fixed on the visor mirror. The red lights were no closer.

Joshua slowed down.

I threw him a look of panic. What was he going to do? Then I saw a turnoff ahead — an unpaved road on the right that disappeared behind a hill about a mile away. Joshua slowed more, but not nearly enough to make the turn. What was he *thinking*? I gripped the edge of my seat and the dashboard, bracing myself. We neared the turnoff. My heart jumped into my throat. I dug my heels against the floor and squeezed my eyes shut.

The car whipped to the right.

I felt us skid … rise up on two wheels. The seconds dragged out. In my mind I saw us flipping over and over. My mouth opened with a keening cry. Here it came, the churning —

The car jolted back onto all four tires.

Our rear end skidded out, then righted.

The Camry leapt forward.

My eyes opened. The hill was straight ahead, still some distance away. Sirens sounded behind us. I looked in the mirror and saw *two* police cars. They'd gained on us when we slowed.

But they would have to make that turn too.

The road curved toward the left of the hill. Joshua didn't slow. His face was red, and his jaw hard and set. I saw the truth in his face — he would never let me get out of this alive. He'd come this far. He had no intention of losing now.

The sirens faded. The police cars had slowed to turn.

We rounded the hill. About a half mile away the road ended. I saw two cabins and a barn.

Joshua let out a growl of victory. His lips spread in a sneering smile.

We rocketed toward the cabins. At the last possible second Joshua slowed. Even then I thought it was too late. We weren't going to stop. We'd go right through one of the buildings.

He hit the brake. An antilock system kicked the car into a crazy shudder. I closed my eyes again and hung on, melting into my seat. Waiting for the crash …

The Camry slung to a stop.

My lungs wouldn't work. I heaved a shuddering sob.

"Get out!" Joshua yelled. "Now!" He undid his seat belt, grabbed his gun, and bolted from the car. I fumbled with my own belt. My fingers wouldn't work. Joshua ran around the front, jerked open my door. My seat belt fell away. He grabbed me by the arm and pulled me out. Shoved me toward the cabin. "Inside!"

I stumbled up one cement block step, Joshua beside me. We crossed a narrow porch with no roof. Joshua flung open the front door, pushed me over the threshold, and jumped in behind me. The door slammed. He locked it.

Joshua dragged me through a rustic living area, a kitchen on our left. Down a central hallway. We passed a bedroom on the right, a bathroom on the left. He sent me sprawling through the second right-hand door. I hit the end of a double bed and collapsed upon it. "Stay there!" He pointed a thick finger at me, then disappeared.

I struggled toward the head of the bed and drew my knees up to my chest.

Joshua's footsteps drummed the cabin's bare floors. I heard a door open, the rattle of something.

Guns?

Sweat beaded on my forehead and ran down my temple.

More running — toward the front of the cabin. Then came an unmistakable sound. A shotgun being cocked.

Footfalls. Joshua appeared in the doorway, shotgun in his left hand. His eyes were narrowed and mean, his lips curling. "They *ain't* takin' you."

We stared at each other.

"Where's Caleb?" My mouth barely worked.

"I don't know."

"Is that his cabin next door?"

"He ain't there. No car out front."

Thank God. If there were two of them ... "Does he have guns too?"

Joshua stabbed me with a look. "We got plenty of protection."

Sirens wailed through the air. Our heads jerked toward the sound. I cringed against the wall. "What are you going to do?"

"*Kill* 'em. And if they send more, kill them too."

My heart curled up and dried out. How many more people were going to die because of me? "Just let me go. Then no one else has to get hurt."

Joshua crossed the space between us in a split second. He grabbed the front of my shirt with one hand and yanked me up in his face. His nose touched mine, and his foul breath spilled over me. "I. Will. *Never*. Let you go. Got that?" He pulled his head back and shook me. My body bounced around. "You're *mine*."

I shrank away. Joshua wouldn't let go of me.

Suddenly, a tiny trickle of courage leaked into my heart. I forced myself to lean toward him. Feigned a concerned look. "They'll kill you."

Joshua's mouth twisted. He stared into my soul with an expression of pure, selfish evil. "Ain't nobody else gonna have you, Shaley. If I die, I'm takin' you with me."

He pushed me back against the wall and stalked from the room.

Randy Sullivan was sweating through an early-morning workout when his cell went off. Bear's ringtone. Randy snatched up the phone. "Crooner."

"We got ourselves a second chance with Shaley O'Connor."

Excitement shot through Randy. "You're kidding. Where is she?"

"In a cabin in north Montana."

Randy's SWAT team served all of Utah, Idaho, and Montana. "They *sure* this time?"

"She's there. Fledger too. Local and state police have them surrounded. Fledger's not communicating. I want you at the Stable in ten minutes. Immediate aerial transport to the scene; we'll brief on the way. Get moving."

The line went dead.

In sixty seconds Randy was gunning his car away from the gym.

Ronald Fledger! We have you surrounded." The voice from the bullhorn echoed between the cabin and the nearby hill. "Come out with your hands on your head. Nobody will get hurt."

I cringed at one end of a worn blue couch in the cabin's living room. I'd heard the voice for almost two hours now. The man had identified himself as Rick Schwartz with the state police. Joshua paced the room, from couch to kitchen and back again. His right hand gripped the shotgun, every movement jerking with tension. His curses mingled with prayers to God to save him.

On the kitchen table lay three handguns. All fully loaded.

How many policemen were outside now? Joshua had closed the cheap white curtains. I had only sound to go by — and I'd heard plenty. Cars arriving, doors slamming.

Joshua halted abruptly and turned accusing eyes on me. "This is all your fault."

I swallowed. "If I go out there — "

"If you weren't such a *celebrity*." He spat the word. "Picture all over the place. Strutting around with that mother of yours."

Oh, *no*, he didn't. Joshua could say what he wanted about me, but not my mom. She would be dying with worry by now.

"Just let me go, Joshua. This'll all be o — "

"Shut up. Shut *up*!" He stalked over and glared down at me. Evil and blame twisted his face.

With a low growl in his throat, he raised the shotgun and pointed it at my head.

I stared at him, heart pounding. This was it. He was going to pull the trigger.

"Ronald Fledger!"

Joshua whirled toward the sound, both arms thrust into the air. "Shut uuuuuupp!" he bellowed. He waved the gun and stomped toward the front door. "Shut up or she's dead!"

The bullhorn fell silent. Had they heard him?

He swiveled back toward me. "You've done this to me! A prophet of God!"

I bit my lip, barely daring to breathe. I had never seen Joshua this unstable. Trapped, he'd become a raving madman.

How to rationalize with someone like that? How to save my own life?

You won't be saved, Shaley. Joshua had meant what he said. If they stormed the cabin, he'd kill me.

A *whop-whop* sounded overhead. Helicopter. I'd heard it on and off.

I thrust a hand in my straggly hair. It had long ago fallen from the rubber-banded ponytail. My scalp felt oily and sweaty. The bruises on my face were purple and black. My arms and hands were also still bruised, and the skin around my wrists remained raw.

What a way to die.

My eyes closed, and in my mind I saw my own broken body lying next to Joshua's.

No.

The voice came from deep within me, barely audible, yet firm.

Don't give up.

I opened my eyes. Watched crazy Joshua resume his stomping back and forth. *Then you'd better help me, God. Because I've got nothing left in me.*

The *whop-whop* beat the air above the cabin, as if the helicopter hovered over us. Joshua stopped near the kitchen table, tipped his head up. He smacked the shotgun into both hands and pointed it at the ceiling.

"No, don't!" The cry burst from me before I could stop it. Joshua pivoted toward me. My hands dug into the couch cushions, my throat going dry. I gulped a breath. "If you shoot, they'll come running in here. They *will*, Joshua. They'll think you're shooting at *me*."

"Maybe I will."

"Do you want to die? Do you *really* want to die?"

He lowered the gun, suddenly looking like a lost child. "They won't go away. They won't leave me *alone*."

My head nodded. "We need to talk to them. I can tell them to back off."

"I'm *not* letting you go out there."

"I can shout through a window."

"No."

"Please. Just let me talk to them."

"*No*."

But his shoulders slumped a little more.

I pushed to my feet.

"Stay there!" He brandished the shotgun at me. "Sit down."

My foot took a step. Was I moving it? "I'm going to the window. I'll tell them to go away."

"*Don't* go near the window."

I took another step. "They're not going to hurt me, Joshua. But you need to stay out of sight. You can be at the wall right next to me."

My legs moved me forward. Joshua watched me, indecision crisscrossing his face. His tongue poked out and licked his upper lip. He pointed the shotgun at me. "You tell them what I say."

"Okay. I will."

I reached the front wall, a few feet from the window. My legs shook. I turned to Joshua. "Don't stand there in the middle of the room."

He moved to the wall on the other side of the front door. His legs were apart, his weapon trained on me. "Open the curtain."

In that instant I pictured dozens of men out there, guns pointed at the cabin. They probably had sharpshooters. One move of the curtain, and all those weapons would swing toward the window.

What if they shot before they saw who it was?

This was crazy. I couldn't do it.

"Open it!" Joshua's face reddened.

"I ... what if they shoot?"

"Shove your face against the window. They'll see it's you."

Maybe. Maybe not. What if the sun glared against the glass?

My knees turned watery. Another minute and I would fall over. As if it belonged to someone else, my hand reached toward the center of the window. I grasped the curtain on my side. Pushed it back.

Dead silence outside. I knew they'd seen the movement. Every eye was now trained on that window.

"Go!" Joshua pushed the air with his left hand.

I thrust myself toward the window. Pressed my face up to the glass. "Go away!" I yelled as loudly as I could. "I don't want you here!"

Joshua pressed against the wall, panting. "Say it again."

"I want to live here!" My left palm raised to the window. "Just leave us alone!"

Nauseating fear spiraled through me. I yanked away from the window. My feet stumbled back until I caught myself.

Silence.

My eyes locked with Joshua's.

"Shaley, we hear you." Schwartz's voice rolled across the cabin. "Let's talk some more. We can get you a two-way radio. Then we won't have to shout."

I nodded at Joshua, silently pleading. If we could talk to them, maybe they'd calm him down. At least distract him. Maybe ... something.

"I got nothin' to say to them," Joshua hissed.

"Then I'll talk." Somehow I kept my voice steady. "I'll keep telling them I want to live here with you. That I'm happy. I can't do it all through a window, Joshua."

"I ain't lettin' anybody come in here. Soon as that door opens, they'll shoot."

Some force outside myself pushed me back to the glass. "How do we get the radio?" I yelled. "We don't want anyone near the cabin!"

"And you're not goin' outside, neither." Joshua took a step closer.

"Just a minute, Shaley," the bullhorn said.

Silence. Barely breathing, I stayed at the window. *Come on, come on.* Joshua could change his mind in a heartbeat.

"Shaley." The voice echoed. "We'll lower it to you from the chopper. Right outside your door. All you have to do is open the door and pull it inside."

"No!" Joshua's left fist bashed against the wall. "We ain't openin' the door!"

"How else are we going to get it in here?"

"We won't. Forget it."

"Joshua, if we say no, at some point every one of them will come barreling in here. We have to convince them to go."

"No."

I turned back toward the window and shouted, "Okay, lower it!" Immediately I pulled back and slid the curtain shut.

Joshua let loose a string of curses. "What'd you do that for?" He stalked toward me, fire in his eyes. "I'm just gonna kill you right now."

"Fine." My throat tightened. I wanted to back away but held my ground. He stopped inches from me. "Then you'll be all alone, with nothing to stop them from forcing their way in here."

"I'm *not* opening that door!" His face turned crimson.

"Then that radio will sit! Just because it's out there doesn't mean we have to get it."

We glared at each other.

Overhead the beat of helicopter wings receded.

Joshua looked up. "It's going away." Anxiety edged the words.

"To pick up the radio."

His chin jerked back down. He pinned me with a stare that iced my veins. "This better work. You better convince them to leave."

I held his gaze, fists pressed against my thighs. "I will."

Joshua backed off. I eased across the room and half fell onto the couch.

We waited.

Joshua resumed pacing. Outside all was quiet. My nerves felt like sawdust. Suddenly I didn't want the radio. Once we had it, I'd have to keep up my act. I'd have to think clearly, keep one step ahead of Joshua. Where would I find the energy?

I didn't want to think about that. I pulled my thoughts away, turned them to Mom and Dad. Brittany and the band. Even if I got out of here alive, what would my life be like? How do you go back to living normally after something like this? Only God would get me through it.

The air above the cabin beat a *thwap-thwap*. The helicopter was back.

Only then did I realize why the police were giving us the radio this way. Even in all the protective gear they surely wore, no one was going to take the chance of walking up to the front door.

Joshua stood like a rock in the middle of the room, gun in his hand and feet apart. He caught my eye, and his mouth pulled into his now familiar threatening sneer.

I know, my expression told him. *I know*.

Something heavy fell on the porch.

Joshua pivoted and aimed his gun at the door.

Long seconds ticked by. The *thwap-thwap* continued — then faded.

"Shaley!" Schwartz's voice came over the bullhorn. "We've left the radio on the porch, two feet from the door."

Joshua strode to the couch and yanked me to my feet. Left hand clamped around my burning wrist, he pulled me to the kitchen table. He tossed down the shotgun and picked up the weapon he'd used to shoot the policeman. Joshua moved behind me and wrapped his left arm around my chest. Dragged me over to the front door.

The gun pressed into my skull beneath my right ear. "When I tell you to, you open the door. When you lean down to get that radio, this gun stays at your head. Got it? One funny move from them and you're dead."

I managed a nod.

"You move real fast." Joshua's arm squeezed against my lungs. I gasped for air. "Unbolt the door, get the radio, get back in. Hear me?"

"Uhh … huh."

The gun barrel dug deeper into my head. "On the count of three."

Please, out there, don't shoot.

Why had I pushed this? It was insane. I was going to *die*.

"One. Two. Three — *go!*"

My hand unbolted the lock. Opened the door. Sunlight poured over me, so bright I could barely see. In a split second my eyes grazed over too many vehicles to count. I leaned down toward the radio, Joshua moving with me. A long rope was tied around the radio. Is that what we'd heard drop? My fingers snatched up the bundle. We backed inside the cabin, a large section of the rope trailing at my feet. Joshua pulled me around the corner and out of sight. I tried to slam the door, but the rope still lay over the threshold.

"Get it!" Joshua yelled.

I reached down with my left hand, trying to reel it in. I couldn't see the end of it. In my mind I envisioned men running toward the door. They'd get me *killed*. Panicked, I pulled harder. The last of the rope whipped toward me.

Joshua leapt around me and slammed the door. Bolted it.

I sank to my knees, then collapsed on the floor, heart flailing.

Joshua grabbed the radio. He fumbled with it, searching for a *talk* button. Raised it to his mouth. "Schwartz. You there?"

From the floor I watched him, too shaken to get up.

"I'm here, Ronald." The voice came through loud, startling.

"My name ain't Ronald, it's Joshua!"

"All right. Joshua."

He flicked me a menacing look. "Shaley's got somethin' to say to you." He thrust the radio toward me. I took it with a trembling hand.

"Shaley?" Schwartz's voice.

"Yeah. I'm here." I ran the back of my hand across my sweaty forehead. *You can do this, Shaley.* "I want you all to go away. I want to stay with Joshua."

Silence.

Joshua grabbed my hair. "Tell 'em again."

My finger keyed the radio. "I ... do you hear me? You all need to leave. I —"

Joshua wrenched the radio from my hands. "Hey! You get that? You have one hour to get every last person outta here. *One hour.* If you ain't gone by then — she dies."

44

Rayne's body felt tight, her lungs parched for air. She walked the great room, unable to stop. They'd watched the horrific scene unfolding on TV until Rayne had to turn away. Those rustic cabins in the middle of nowhere, police cars littering the road, men in gear carrying multiple weapons. The news was being broadcast courtesy of the closest TV station crew, who'd rushed to the scene. Rayne knew other local and national crews were on their way from all points in the country. Let them film all they wanted. She couldn't bear to watch.

Ross, Ed Schering, Morrey, and Kim remained in the den, eyes glued to the TV. They would report if they saw anything new.

Rayne paced. Every minute was torture, every ring of Al's phone a nightmare waiting to unfold. Brittany, Gary, and the rest of the band had gathered in the great room, their official location to wait. No one spoke. The very air twanged with tension.

An hour ago Al had received a call about John Baynor, the man who owned the Utah cabin where Shaley had been taken the first night. Baynor had stumbled into the police station in Lewistown, Montana, frightened and shaking, and spilled his story to a detective. Al related the information to Rayne and Gary.

"He and Ronald Fledger built cabins outside of Peace, Montana, planning on starting some sort of religious community. The kind cut off from the world — no phones, no TV. Baynor stayed at the place while Fledger left, saying he'd come back as soon as possible with his 'bride.' Baynor insisted he had no idea about Fledger's plans to kidnap Shaley."

Gary huffed. "His Utah cabin sure was convenient. The electricity was even left on."

Stan and Rich crowded in, listening. Brittany gripped Carly's hand.

Al shrugged. "He says his brother was going to move into the Utah place. At any rate, Baynor happened to go into Peace yesterday. In a diner he saw Fledger's face on TV, wanted for kidnapping Shaley. Baynor says he ran out of the restaurant and took off south. He didn't want any part of that. He stayed in Lewistown last night, and this morning on TV saw the news about the Montana cabins being surrounded. That's when he went to the police."

Rayne pressed her hands to her temples. "Will he talk to Fledger? Try to convince him to let Shaley go?"

Police were flying him to the scene, Al had said. Baynor was going to try.

The latest news from Al was that Baynor had arrived at the Montana cabins. A few minutes later a radio was delivered to Fledger. Now at least the police could communicate with him.

Al's phone went off again. Rayne pulled up short and swiveled toward the sound. Gary strode over to the FBI agent.

"Scarrow." Al's eyes met Rayne's across the room. He listened.

Rayne's fingers laced so tightly they cramped. *What is it, what is it?* She walked toward him, part of her wanting to back away. To not hear.

"Thanks." Al punched off the line.

"What?" Gary demanded.

"They've talked to Shaley. She's insisting she wants them to go away and leave her alone."

Gary's face reddened. "He's making her say that!"

"We know." Al looked from him to Rayne, hesitating. Fear whirled through Rayne. Whatever it was, he didn't want to tell them.

"Fledger's given an ultimatum. The police must leave in one hour."

"Or what?" Gary's face paled.

"No!" Rayne's knees sagged. "Don't say it." She sank into the nearest chair. "Just ... don't."

45

From my place on the couch, I eyed the two-way radio sitting on the coffee table, useless and silent. Joshua had quit talking to Schwartz, and now he didn't want me near the thing. "Nothin' left to do but count down the hour," he'd told me. "There's no halfway about this. Either they leave or they don't."

And what if they do go, Joshua? I wanted to ask. Did he really think they'd just leave me here, a kidnap victim, forever? My guess — he *knew* they wouldn't leave. He was just buying time. Otherwise, why give them an hour? Why not demand they leave in five minutes?

Joshua didn't dare get near a window to see what was happening outside. One sighting of him, and a sniper would shoot in an instant. He'd given an ultimatum, and he couldn't even check to see if it was being followed.

He was trapped. He didn't know what to do. Somehow I had to use that.

But I hadn't gotten a chance. Minutes streamed by, and Joshua grew more volatile than ever. By now the hour had to be almost gone. The man couldn't stop pacing. His limbs trembled and jerked as if hooked up to electrodes. His right hand gripped a handgun. Any second he might explode. Just pivot and shoot me. Joshua cursed Caleb for abandoning him; he cursed me. Finally he cursed God. After a while my ears grew so used to his verbal abuse I barely heard it. My body sank in on itself, wrapped in cotton. I tried to tell myself I wasn't really there. I was … somewhere else. Drifting. This was all a dream.

Joshua strode to the coffee table and slapped a hand around the radio. "Hey, Schwartz!" His eyes fastened on me as he talked. They were flat and hard. At that moment I knew it was over.

"Schwartz here, Joshua."

"You got five minutes."

"According to my watch we have fifteen."

"I just moved it up. I'm *tired* of this."

"There's someone here wants to talk to you. Just a minute."

I didn't dare move.

"Joshua." A new voice crackled over the radio. "It's Caleb."

Joshua cursed and threw the radio on the table. "I ain't talkin' to that Judas."

I cringed on the couch and studied Joshua, pulse skimming. Caleb's voice had thrown him.

You've got five minutes.

"I'll talk to him." I pushed to the edge of the sofa.

"No, you ain't!"

"Let me find out why he abandoned us."

Us. Joshua gave me a long look. His lip curled. *Us.* I could see the effect that word had on him. He wanted Caleb to hear my loyalty.

Joshua shrugged.

I leaned over and picked up the radio. "Caleb, it's Shaley. You here — outside?"

"I came back to talk to Joshua."

"We want to know why you left."

"Why do you think? I didn't know he was going to kidnap you."

I locked eyes with Joshua. "That how you treat your friends? Just up and ditch them?"

"I didn't want any part in what he did."

Silence. I waited him out, envisioning Schwartz standing nearby, telling Caleb what to say. What a game of chess we played. With my life at stake.

"Get Joshua on the radio," Caleb said.

I stood and held out the radio to Joshua. He cursed again and turned away.

"Come on, Joshua. Here's your chance to tell him what a traitor he is."

No response.

"I want to hear you tell him. I want to hear the kind of man you are."

My captor's gaze cut back to me, his eyes narrowed and cold. His mouth tightened. He closed the gap between us and whisked the radio from my hand. "I'm here, Caleb, so whad'ya want?"

"I want you to come out of there. You think I want to see you killed?"

"Ain't nobody killin' me. They all got to leave *now*."

"They'll leave for sure if you come out."

Joshua's face turned crimson. "*I am not giving up!* They leave now or Shaley dies. You tell them that!"

I sidled toward the front window.

"There's no good can come of this, Joshua."

"I ain't goin' to jail!"

"Why would you go to jail? I thought Shaley wants to be with you."

"You heard her."

"Then come on out with her. She wants to stay with you, you can be together. Don't have to be holed up in that cabin."

I reached the window. Stepped just beyond it and edged aside the curtain an inch. My line of vision cut diagonally across the yard.

"What're you doin'?" Joshua bellowed.

My insides shook, but I didn't let the curtain fall. "Checking outside. Stay where you are, they can't see you." I pushed my face toward the glass.

"Close it!"

"I see him." My eyes raked over the police cars. No sign of a man who could be Caleb. "He's just standing out in the yard, nobody around him. Like he trusts you. He knows you won't shoot him."

Joshua snorted. "Man that stupid won't live long."

Motion down the road caught my attention. I leaned a little to the right. More cars rolled toward the cabin. And a huge armored vehicle some distance behind them.

Did they want to get me killed?

I licked my lips. Glanced at Joshua.

"What's Caleb doing?" He took a step in my direction.

"He's waving at me," I said in a rush. *"Don't* come any closer. The police cars are still out there."

Joshua pulled the radio close to his mouth. "Hey, out there! You got five minutes. Hear me? The hour's up in *five minutes.*"

The cars drove up a little more and stopped. The armored vehicle stopped too but remained about thirty feet from the cars. Maybe they didn't want to bring it any nearer for fear of being heard. A thing like that had to make a lot of noise. Men in camouflage gear and vests, carrying large weapons, piled out of the cars. They made no sound.

SWAT team.

Part of me couldn't believe it. This should be Brittany and me watching a cop movie. Eating popcorn. I couldn't really be here. *In* this.

"What's he doing now?" Joshua smacked the gun against his leg.

I peered out the window. "He's talking to people behind the police cars. I can't see them. I think he's telling them to leave."

"That's right, Caleb," Joshua spat into the radio. "You tell 'em to *go.*"

I left the window and trotted over to Joshua's side. If he found out I was lying, he would shoot me in an instant. "Give me the radio."

"No."

"I can watch them out the window and talk. You can't."

Suspicion creased Joshua's face. "I got to see for myself."

"How? They see you, they shoot you."

He studied me, unsure.

"Come on, Joshua!" I reached for the radio.

He handed it over.

I swiveled away and ran back to the window before he could

change his mind. Lifted up the outer edge of a curtain. "Caleb, it's Shaley. I see you in the yard. You were talking to the police. You telling them to leave?"

The SWAT team men were bent over, running in different directions.

Please get what I'm doing.

"Yeah, Shaley." Caleb's voice crackled. "I'm telling 'em to go. I'll stay. Joshua and I can talk. We'll figure out what to do."

"I got nothin' to say to him," Joshua retorted.

Two SWAT team members were headed straight for the front door. *The front door!* Others moved toward each side of the cabin. That bedroom I'd been in had a back window.

A tremble started in the soles of my feet. Moved up to my ankles. *If I die, I'm takin' you with me, Shaley.* I resisted the urge to glance at all the weapons on the kitchen table. The gun in Joshua's hand was enough. One noise from those back bedrooms and I was dead. I knew that. Looking at Joshua, seeing the craziness in his eyes — I didn't stand a chance.

"Shaley." Caleb's voice.

I could stop this charade right now. Stop the gamble on my life. *And then what?*

"Shaley?"

"Shut him up!" Joshua barked.

My shaking finger slipped as I keyed the radio. "I'm here." I could barely hear my own words. Blood whooshed in my ears.

"You see them getting in their cars?"

Policemen emerged from behind the vehicles. Slid inside the cars and slammed doors. I turned to Joshua. "Hear that?"

He cocked his head, listening.

More policemen got into the cars that had just brought the SWAT team. Engines started up. They began to move — away from the cabin and down the road. Even the armored car made a wide turn and rolled away.

They wouldn't have to go far. Just around the hill.

"They're leaving." My voice trembled. "They really are going. Only our car's left."

"I got to check." Joshua strode toward the window in the kitchen. "You see anybody with Caleb?"

"I don't even see Caleb. I think he moved behind the Camry."

"Yeah, him and who else?"

No reply from me.

"Tell him to stand up and put his hands in the air."

It was so quiet outside. Where were all those SWAT men? Was Schwartz behind the Camry with Caleb, still telling him what to say?

"Caleb, Joshua wants to see you. Stand up behind the car and put your hands up."

A pause. "What for? So he can shoot me?"

"He wants to see you don't have a gun in your hand. He's not going to shoot you."

"How do I know that?"

I pierced Joshua with a look. He gripped the handgun, his teeth clenched and wildness on his face. My heart smacked against my ribs. I lowered the radio. "You're not going to shoot him, are you? Everyone has left. There's no point."

He aimed the gun straight at my head. "I just want to see that they're gone."

I had to let them know where Joshua was.

I raised the radio to my lips. "He won't shoot, Caleb. Just look toward the other front window."

Joshua's gun remained pointed at me. I had to make this happen.

"Okay," Caleb said. "I'm standing up. See? Nothing in my hands except the radio."

I swallowed hard, nodded to Joshua. *Do it!*

He turned his gun away from me, positioned himself at the edge of the window — and edged back the curtain.

Gunfire exploded. The front door blew open.

46

Randy stormed into the cabin, Bray, Rex, Bear, Volt, and Eagle stacked behind him. Glass broke toward the back of the building. Starsky and Coop breaching the rear window.

Randy pivoted left. From the corner of his eye he saw Shaley. She screamed and fell to the floor.

The HT reeled back from the window. He hit the wall hard, a gun falling from his hand. Randy's shouts blended with his team's. "On the ground, on the ground!"

Fledger lunged toward a table loaded with weapons.

Randy aimed his gun. "On the ground *now*!"

The HT's hand launched out, scrabbled for a gun.

47

Deafening gunfire burst through the cabin. I curled into a ball on the floor, arms over my head. The whole world was breaking apart.

The seconds jarred into slow motion. I heard men's shouts. More gunfire. I twisted my head toward the kitchen window. Saw Joshua slam back against the wall. His arms came up. One wrist hit the window frame, the other smacked into the edge of a cabinet. Horror and shock gripped his face. His glazed eyes cut toward me.

For a final split instant we stared at each other.

Joshua's eyes rolled back in his head. His arms fell. He collapsed to his knees and onto his side.

Men ran toward him.

Joshua twitched. Then lay still.

The world spun.

It couldn't have happened so fast. After the last two horrible days? I'd dreamed this rescue. Any minute now Joshua would wake me up, drag me out of the cabin. Tell me what to do, where to go. Hit me if I didn't obey ...

Darkness closed around me. A sea swept me out ... away ...

"Shaley." A man's voice seeped into my senses. Not Joshua's. "Shaley."

Hands on my shoulders. A gentle shake. "Shaley. It's okay now."

My eyes opened. A man knelt over me, dressed in camouflage and a thick bulletproof vest. A helmet lay on the floor beside him.

He had dark hair and large, dark eyes. The kindest face I'd ever seen in my life.

My mouth moved. No words came.

He smiled. "It's okay now. It's okay."

"Who — who are you?"

"I'm Randy. We came to help you."

Randy. The SWAT team.

All the memories flooded back. And the fear. I gripped Randy's sleeve. "Where's Joshua?"

Randy shook his head. "He won't hurt you anymore."

Relief and elation and exhaustion swept through me like a tidal wave. I sat up and threw my arms around Randy. Burst into wild sobs. "Thank you, thank you!"

He stroked my hair. "It's okay. It's okay."

The sobs kept coming. I couldn't let go of him, and I couldn't stop crying.

I sensed other men crowding around. Heard voices in radios. "It's done. HT's taken out. Hostage is fine."

A new thought spiraled through me. I pulled away from Randy. Tipped my face up to his. "I want to talk to my mom!"

PART 4
Saturday, Four Weeks Later

48

Through teary eyes I watched Mom walk down the aisle in her stunning wedding dress, escorted by Ross and Stan. Her face was radiant, full of love for my dad. He stood waiting at the front of the huge church, hands clasped in front of him, a wavering smile on his lips. I knew he was trying not to cry.

The church was packed with our friends, old and new. Every person who'd helped find me had been invited. Agent Scarrow, his FBI team, the Utah State Police members who'd tried to rescue me from the first cabin. Ed and Jean Carroll, whose trailer Joshua had broken into. And the SWAT team.

Unable to forget the terrible days they'd spent at Ed Schering's mansion, Mom and Dad had chosen this church in Southern California for the wedding. But they'd taken their time. I'd needed a new bridesmaid dress. And we'd wanted a month's healing behind us — both emotionally and physically. I'd told them everything that had happened to me. They and the FBI had been surprised to hear some of the details, like the car trunk Joshua had put me in after the van. They hadn't even known about that vehicle. As for my bruises, they'd turned from purple and black to greenish yellow, finally fading, then disappearing completely.

My gaze slid from Mom toward a pew she'd just passed, where Randy Sullivan sat with his wife. He caught my eye and smiled. My eyes burned all the more. I clamped my mouth together and nodded.

"I've been dreaming of this day my entire life!"

Four weeks ago I'd said that to my mom. Now the day was finally coming true.

"She's so beautiful," Brittany whispered beside me.

"I know." Underneath my bouquet, I rubbed Dad's ring, stuck on my forefinger.

All eyes were on Mom, but she could only look at the man she loved.

My thoughts flashed back to the day I was rescued. To driving toward Peace with Rick Schwartz until we picked up a phone signal. Calling my mom on his cell. I remembered the moment I first heard her voice. I slumped toward the dashboard, crying and crying. Mom sobbed too. Then Dad was on the line. He couldn't even talk except for one word. "Shaley ... Shaley ... Shaley."

I threw him a look across the aisle. He was fixated on Mom. His clasped hands fidgeted with excitement.

Thank you, God. Thank you.

The three of us had done a lot of talking since our reunion. About God, and how he cares for us, even while allowing trouble to come into our lives. That was the hardest part to understand—why God let everything happen. Still, in the end our prayers had been answered.

Mom, Stan, and Ross reached the front pew. A few more steps and they neared Gary.

"Who gives this woman to this man?" the black-robed preacher asked.

"*I* do." Ross spoke the words with animation. His eyebrows rose. This was his moment, and he was going to make the most of it. "I do."

"And *I* do!" Stan said even louder.

"And me!" I burst out. "And me!"

A chuckle ran through the audience.

Mom threw me a smile. Her eyes said: *Shaley, don't make me cry.*

I watched Ross and Stan place Mom's hand into Dad's and step back. As the entire bridal party turned toward the preacher, tears spilled down my face. I couldn't stop them.

I didn't even want to try.

These discussion questions can be used in a book club (a mother-daughter book club, a teen book club) or even as questions to use with friends also reading this book.

1. When this story opens, it's the happiest day of Shaley's life. What has been your happiest day? Why?

2. If you were Brittany, would you blame yourself for not going with Shaley to get the ring? If your best friend was kidnapped, what would you do?

3. Rayne and Gary are new Christians. Have you ever seen something bad happen to someone soon after he or she became a Christian? How did that person cope?

4. Have you ever really loved someone but couldn't be with them? Imagine you're Rayne or Gary: What would you have felt if your daughter had been taken away?

5. Do you think that Shaley felt as though God had abandoned her when she was kidnapped? Have you ever felt like God abandoned you in your greatest need?

6. Joshua called himself a Christian but didn't act like one at all. Do you know someone like that? If so, how do you interact with this person?

7. In chapter 27, Shaley said that she had no strength to pray, but she had enough to be angry with her captor. Have you ever felt so helpless or been so angry at God that you couldn't pray? How did you deal with those feelings?

8. At the beginning of chapter 36, Shaley is losing hope. If you were her, would you fight back or give up

9. As time passes, Shaley has to take a big risk to get help, one that could get Joshua very angry. Would you have taken the risk she did? Explain.

10. At the end of the book, Shaley concludes it's hard to understand why God allowed her to be kidnapped. Do you ever wonder why God allows things to happen like they do? Do you believe God does everything for a reason?

11. Have you ever met someone that people said couldn't be helped, but you tried to help him or her anyway? Do you think God sent you for that purpose? Why or why not?

12. What part of *Final Touch* was your favorite? Why?

13. What has this story taught you about God?

Many thanks to teens Emily Love, Dylan DeVries, Ashley Harman, and Nicole Blocher for writing discussion questions for *Final Touch*.

the Rayne Tour

ALWAYS WATCHING

BRANDILYN COLLINS
& AMBERLY COLLINS

Read chapter 1 of *Always Watching*, Book 1 in The Rayne Tour.

1

The screams of twenty thousand people sizzled in my ears.

"Rayne, you reign! Rayne, you reign! Rayne, you reign!"

At the sold-out HP Pavilion in San Jose, California, the crowd chanted and clapped and stomped for my mom's group, Rayne — named after her — to do one more song before they left the stage. As usual I stood backstage with Tom Hutchens, my mom's twenty-five-year-old hairdresser and makeup artist and my closest friend on tour. Tom was short and slim, with thick black hair and an intense-looking face that didn't match his crazy personality at all.

Tom feigned the pucker of a hip-hop artist and splayed his fingers in front of his red T-shirt. "Yo, she reign, they go insane!" He had to shout at me, his Vans-clad feet dancing. Tom always wore these wild-looking sneakers with blue, white, and red checks and a red racing stripe on the sides. "Ain't nothin' plain about rockin' Rayne!"

I punched him in the arm, laughing. His silly rap rhymes were getting worse by the day.

With her blonde hair bouncing, Mom came flying down the steps on the way to her private dressing room for the two-minute break. Sweat shone on her forehead as she passed by. She flashed her red-lipped grin at me and raised a palm. We high-fived as she sped past.

"They love us, Shaley!"

"Course, Mom, they always do!"

The rest of the rock group — Kim, Morrey, Rich, and Stan — descended more slowly, their faces showing fatigue. None of them had the energy of my mother after a concert. Tom and I gave them a quick thumbs-up before scurrying after Mom.

As we hit the dressing room with Rayne O'Connor's name on the door, I checked my watch. 10:45. Yay! Almost time to head to the airport and pick up my best friend, Brittany. I hadn't seen her since Rayne started touring three months ago, and I couldn't *wait* to be with her again. This was Rayne's third tour, and I always found it hard to leave all my school friends behind.

Without Tom to keep me laughing, touring would be terribly lonely.

I walked in and closed the dressing room door, shutting out some of the noise.

"Whoo!" Mom crossed to the left side of the room and plopped into the makeup chair facing a long, brightly lit mirror. To her right sat a wooden armoire full of her clothing. She always changed outfits during intermission. Along the back wall were the blue sofa and matching armchairs specified by contract for her dressing area in every arena. Opposite the makeup counter was the table loaded with catered food, also specified by contract — bowls of fruit, sandwiches, pasta salad, cheese cubes, chips … and M&M's for me.

Mom studied herself in the mirror with her large crystal blue eyes. "Okay, Tom, do your magic." She guzzled a drink from a water bottle on the counter.

Like she needed any magic. With her high cheekbones, oval face, and full lips, Mom was drop-dead gorgeous.

Tom winked at me as he snatched up a tissue. Sticking his

scrawny neck out, he scrutinized Mom with animation — eyes narrowed and his mouth a rounded O. "Hm. Hmm."

He sighed, stood back, and spread his hands as if to say *nothing to be done here, you're perfect.*

Mom rolled her eyes at me. I shrugged. As if I could control Tom's antics.

"All right, lover boy." Mom took another swig of water. "Get to it! I've got one minute left."

"Yo, big Mama."

Mom swatted his hand. "Would you stop calling me that? I don't know why I put up with you." Her mouth curved.

Tom leaned in to blot her face with the tissue. "'Cause I make you look bodacious, that's why." Expertly, he retouched her blusher and lipstick and fluffed her hair.

Out in the arena, the crowd's yells and applause were growing louder. I smiled and squeezed Mom's shoulder. At every concert the fans went wild, but it never got old for me. Night after night their adoration made my chest swell with pride for my mom.

Five years ago when I was eleven and Mom was twenty-eight, Rayne was barely hanging on. Mom and the band played little concerts here and there, working night and day to get noticed. I remember how hard she tried back then. A great lyric writer with a distinct, throaty-edged voice, she deserved to make it big. Then the song "Far and Near" hit the radio, and after that — a rocket launch.

Tom stood back and surveyed Mom, his head cocked to one side. "Not bad. Not bad a-tall."

"Rayne, you reign! Rayne, you reign!" The crowd was going crazy out there.

Mom tossed her hair back and looked at herself from side to side. "Great." She sprang from the chair. "Gotta go." She hurried toward the door.

I moved out of her way. "Mom, don't forget, Tom and I are going

to pick up Brittany in ten minutes. We're leaving a little early because Tom wants to stop by a drugstore."

"Oh, that's right." Mom pulled up short, one hand on the door
knob. She looked to Tom. "Somebody else doing your cleanup?"

He glanced at me. "Got it taken care of."

Disappointment pulled at my mouth. Mom *knew* how I'd
counted the days until Brittany's and my junior year of high school
ended — just yesterday. My tutor had flown home this morning, and
now Brittany was coming for two weeks. Mom was paying all her
expenses — for that I was so grateful. But Mom could get so wrapped
up in her work. Sometimes I just needed her to remember *me*.

Mom looked my way — and caught my expression. She smiled
too wide, as if to make up for her distraction. "I'm so glad Brittany's
coming, Shaley. We'll show her a great time."

I nodded.

"Mick's going with you, right?"

"Yeah."

Mick Rader had been my mom's main personal bodyguard for
the past three years. The other two, Bruce Stolz and Wendell Ben-
nington, would guard her on her way to the hotel tonight while
Mick was with me.

"Okay, good. You'll be safe." Mom smiled as she opened the
door. The crowd's screams rushed in. "See you at the hotel."

She blew me a kiss and disappeared.

The yelling suddenly frayed my nerves. I pushed the door shut
and leaned against it.

Tom shot me his sad clown look, his lips turned down and
eyebrows pulled into a V. He always read my mind so well.

I couldn't help but smile. "It's okay."

His expression whisked away. Tom struck his hip-hop pose.
"Got a new one for ya."

"Oh, yeah?" I knew he'd come up with the lyrics as he went
along, just to get me laughing again.

Tom's feet started their shuffle-dance. "Let's go for a ride down the avenue. Top down, windblown, my VW. The talk of the town in all we do. Shaley O'Connor puttin' on the view—"

He froze, mouth open, frowning hard. Then he jerked back into dancing. "Can't think of another line, can you?"

I giggled. "Great, Tom, as fabulous as all your others."

He bowed. "Thank ya, thank yaaa."

Pulling up straight, he glanced at the wall clock. "Yikes! I gotta take care of some things before the limo comes. Meet you at the back exit?"

"Okay."

As the door closed behind him, I crossed the room to check myself in the mirror. Excitement pulsed through my veins. Almost time to see Brittany! I chose a neutral lipstick and leaned toward the glass to apply it. Thanks to Tom, I'd learned a lot of makeup tricks, and my face needed little retouching. Finished with the lipstick, I ran a brush through my long brown hair. Tom had recently layered it and feathered the bangs. I liked the look.

Despite the difference in hair color, many people said I looked like my mother. I considered that a high compliment.

I stood back and turned side to side. Not bad. My new designer jeans fit well, and the blue top matched my eyes. Brittany would love the outfit. I grinned at myself, then glanced at the clock. Almost time for the limo to arrive.

In the arena, the crowd roared. Rayne was taking the stage. The first of two encore songs started—the band's new hit, "Do It Up Right."

For a few minutes I paced the room impatiently, munching M&M's. Rayne launched into their final song of the night.

Two hard knocks sounded on the door—Mick's signal. He stuck his square-shaped head inside. Mick is in his forties, ex-military. He has a thick neck and muscles out to *here*. Nobody messes with Mick. "Shaley, you ready?"

"Yes! Is the limo waiting?"

"Yeah." His deep-set brown eyes swept the room. "Where's Tom?"

"He said he had to take care of a few things. He'll meet us at the door." I crossed to the couch to pick up my purse.

"Okay. I'm going to stop in the bathroom, then I'll see you there." He gave me his squinty-eyed stare. "*Don't* step outside of the building without me."

I flicked a look at the ceiling. "Yeah, yeah." Mick was *so* protective. It's not like I'd be in any danger walking out that door. As with all arenas where Rayne sang, the HP Pavilion had a special entrance for performers, guarded by the arena's own local security. And that whole section of the parking lot was roped off and guarded. No chance for any fans or paparazzi to sneak in.

Mick jabbed a finger at me for emphasis, then left.

Tingling with anticipation, I scurried out the door, intent on checking the other dressing rooms for Tom. *No time to wait, let's go, let's go!* Having been at the arena since four o'clock when sound checks began, I'd already learned the layout of the backstage area. There were eight dressing rooms — Mom's the biggest.

I hurried down the wide hall, mouthing "hi" to people I passed. The sound and light crews were still working, but the backline crew — the guys who maintain all the instruments and switch them out during performances — were done now. Set carpenters, managers, and all the people who tore down the stage milled around until the concert ended.

First I went to the back exit and peeked outside. Tom wasn't there.

I returned all the way up the hall, figuring I'd work my way back down.

For the first time, I noticed all the dressing room doors were closed. Strange. If Tom had gone into one to pack up something, he'd have left the door open as a courtesy. Those assigned rooms were personal space to members of the band and Rayne's production manager, Ross Blanke.

I peeked in the one next to Mom's.

Empty.

Shoving my purse handles higher up my shoulder, I went to the third.

Empty again.

The fourth.

No Tom.

This wasn't right. Tom was never late. Where was he?

Mick approached, signaling me with a roll of his finger — *let's get moving.*

I nodded. "Tom wasn't in the bathroom?"

Mick shook his head.

Together we walked to the fifth dressing room. Mick poked his head inside.

Empty.

I ran down to look in the sixth. No Tom.

I banged the door shut and looked around. What was going on? If he didn't show up soon, we wouldn't have time to go out of our way to a drugstore. The airport was minutes away from the arena. We didn't want Brittany waiting around by herself after dark.

"You take the next one." Mick strode past me. "I'll look in the one on the end."

The seventh dressing room had been allocated as Ross's office. At every venue, he needed a private area for calling people, dealing with last-minute problems, and basically seeing that everything in the contract was honored. I couldn't remember seeing Ross in the hall. He might be inside, and I didn't dare just barge in. The production manager's office was off-limits to everyone, unless invited.

I knocked and waited. Knocked harder.

No answer.

I opened the door.

Like Mom, Ross ordered the same room setup each time. For him that included an oversize desk with a black leather chair. On the desk he would stack his papers and folders, carefully position his laptop. A fax machine had to be on his left, a telephone with multiple lines on his right. Looking at Ross — a short, fat man with scraggly hair to his shoulders — you'd never guess what a neat freak he is.

And always on the wall — a large round clock.

As I stepped into the room, my eyes grazed that clock. 10:55. Brittany's plane would be landing soon.

On the floor beside the desk I glimpsed a splash of color.

Something twisted inside my stomach, almost as if my subconscious mind had already registered the sight. Time seemed to slow.

Clutching the door handle, I turned my head toward the color.

A foot. On the floor, sticking out from behind the desk. Wearing a Vans with blue, white, and red checks and a red racing strip. The foot lay on its side, toes pointed away from me, heel dug awkwardly into the carpet.

Deathly still.

The Rayne Tour

by Brandilyn Collins and Amberly Collins!

A suspenseful three-book series for young adults written by bestselling author Brandilyn Collins and her daughter, Amberly. The series is about the daughter of a rock star, life on the road, and her search for her real father.

Always Watching
Book One

This daughter of a rock star has it all — until murder crashes her world.

Last Breath
Book Two

With his last breath, a dying man whispered four stunning words into Shaley O'Connor's ear. Should she believe them?

Final Touch
Book Three

Shaley O'Connor is kidnapped minutes before the long-awaited wedding of her mother and once-estranged father.

Pick up a copy today at your favorite bookstore!

ZONDERVAN®

Want FREE books?
FIRST LOOKS at the best new teen reads?
Awesome EXCLUSIVE video trailers,
contests, prizes, and more?

We want to hear from YOU!

Give us your opinion on titles, covers, and stories.
Join the Z Street Team today!

Visit ZStreetTeam.Zondervan.com to sign up

Connect with us:

 /GoodTeenReads   @GoodTeenReads

ZONDERVAN®
.com